# Nashvegas NIGHTS

## KAT ADDAMS

# 1

## LIZ

Prudence. Dorothy Elizabeth Prudence. That had been my name since birth. I might as well have a tattoo on my forehead, branding me as *unfuckable*. Not that I was actually unfuckable. Because, ya know, I wasn't. Not really anyway. I just hadn't been … shall we say … properly handled … in the history of ever. I'd had lovers, but they were all just *okay*. They had been a little too vanilla and a little too dry—if you catch my drift. Just ho-hum in the sack. And I was so over ho-hum. Life was too short for ho-hum sex. It was a waste of my time, which I didn't have a lot of anymore. My job as a nurse in the ER left me exhilarated, breathless, challenged, and dead tired— which was exactly what I needed in my bed right about now.

"Come on, Liz! We're going to be late! The band starts at ten!" Jessica paced back and forth in front of my bathroom door.

She was always on time. I was not.

It wasn't that I was high maintenance or that I took forever to get ready, but it was my extreme indecisiveness that often led me down the path of: *Oh shit, I'm late again! Which jeans make me have a bubble butt? Do I want a bubble butt tonight? Or do I need a man who is okay with my not-quite bubble butt, not-quite pancake boohiney? Maybe a mix between an apple and a peach? An overripe and slightly squishy one? Am I looking for serious conversations, or am I looking for a good lay?* Those were the important questions. I had to know these things before I left for a night out on the town, and so often, I just couldn't make up my mind.

But tonight was different. I knew what I wanted. I just had to find the perfect outfit to get me there.

*Cleavage? Check.*

*Legs? Check.*

*But not too much legs? Check.*

If I was showing the top, I couldn't be showing the bottom, and vice versa. A girl had to have some class, you know.

*Strappy heels that he can imagine slowly taking off like some romantic Cinderella scene? No.*

That was not what I wanted. Tonight, I needed to get ridden hard and hung out wet to dry.

Come-fuck-me heels. That was what I needed to wear.

Except I would also be drinking and likely break my neck in heels like that.

*Hmm. Blood-red heels for a pop of color against the little black dress?*

"Jess! Does this look okay? What do you think about the heels? Too much?"

"Oh my gosh, lady! You always look great in whatever you wear! You can wear a paper bag, and you'll get fucked tonight." Jess rolled her eyes.

"So, that's a yes on the heels?" I tapped my foot.

"Yes! Of course! Now, let's go. Luke will be here in a second," she said as she stared down into her phone.

Jess was so incredibly lucky. Her husband was the sweetest man. He always offered to be the chauffeur on girls' night. Although playing chauffeur wasn't much of a stretch, considering that they lived in the same neighborhood as me. But still, he was a sweetheart and always looked out for us. I'd watched him hold Jess's hair back one girls' night while she nearly died on the side of the road from one too many tequila shots. I remembered thinking at that time, even drunk, that was what real love looked like—and also that we would never drink tequila again.

"Okay, let's go! I'm ready," I said, dousing myself in the sultriest perfume I owned.

I offered it up to Jess. She waved it away.

She didn't need to get laid—not with her perfect husband and all. She was actually going out because she liked listening to the bands. Me? I couldn't care less about the music. I just needed some stuffin' for this muffin or else I was going to be hangry—and hangry wasn't a good look on me. My poor patients at the ER would feel the brunt of that.

The doorbell rang just as we gathered our things. Luke had arrived.

"You know you can just honk the horn! You don't have to come to the door like a gentleman," I said to him as we hustled out the door and into the car.

"Now, what kind of manners would that be? Honkin' my horn and waking the whole neighborhood? Besides, I like treating ladies like they're supposed to be treated. Gets me in the good graces of this hot piece of ass right here," he said, reaching over to grab Jess, who laughed and gave him a big smooch on the lips.

"All right, you two. Eyes on the road," I said as we pulled out of the driveway. "Besides, doesn't the newlywed stage end after, oh … um … one or two months? You two still can't keep your hands off each other, and it's been, what, four years?"

"Almost five years. And I just can't help it. I mean, look at him!" Jess eye-fucked her husband, who looked back at her and wiggled his brows. "Liz is just getting hangry, Luke. If ya know what I mean. She's on the prowl tonight."

"Is that so? I wondered what you were up to in those red heels."

"So, the red heels are a yes then? They look okay? From a man's perspective? Your wife wasn't much help!" I started to second-guess my choice of attire.

"I'd say they definitely put you on the market for getting your hangry face stuffed, if that's what you're looking for."

"She needs it all stuffed. She's been sooo bitchy lately. Face, muffin, maybe even buns? No, Liz doesn't do that on the first date. I know. Definitely not the buns. *Yet*," Jess teased.

Normally, I would be mortified to talk butt sex, but Jess and I shamelessly talked about everything—and I did mean everything. Some days, we had all the maturity of twelve-year-old boys, making fart jokes, and other days, we held each other as we navigated this adulting world we had been forced into. We were peaches and cream, peanut butter and jelly, Liz and Jess. We were Jess plus Liz, better known as Team Jizz.

"Speaking of buns, I hope you're careful. No buns in the oven, no grease in the pan," Luke said, flinching.

"Grease in the pan? Ew, gross. What does that even mean?" Jess said, fake gagging in disgust.

"Don't know. Just made it up. Like it?" Luke laughed. He was proud of himself for trying to be a part of Team Jizz ... and succeeding.

"That's brilliant!" I snorted. "I'm a smart cookie. I'm not looking to bake buns or ... have a cheesy taco."

"Fuck, that's nasty!" He cringed. "I never knew women could be like y'all until I met you two. You two are something else. Phew, boy. Cheers to Jizz!"

"Cheers to Jizz!" we echoed our mantra as we hopped out of the car and onto Broadway.

"And no tequila!" he called as he blew a kiss in our direction.

"I'm not really sure how he handles us," I said to Jess as she pulled me along to the bar where her favorite band would be playing.

"Luke? Oh, he loves it! He gets to indulge his inner child with us. We're his medicine. Too much corporate stuffiness during the day. But me and you? We make him laugh. He could Jizz all night. Ha!"

"Oh, really? You'll have to tell me all about that—after we get a drink," I said as we made our way to the bar inside the dark and crowded room.

"Two negronis, please," I told the bartender as we settled into two tiny barstools, squished in between a mix of college kids and thirty-somethings trying to be twenty-somethings—which, I shamefully admitted, would be us in a few short years.

"Aww! Thanks, bitch. You know the way to my heart. I'll get the next round," Jess said, patting my knee.

"No way. Your husband is our chauffeur. My treat tonight. Anyway, I owe you."

"For what?"

"For getting me laid tonight," I said matter-of-factly.

"Ha-ha! You know I can definitely help with that. Let's see … who can we seduce tonight?" she said, looking out over the crowd. "How about four o'clock? Beard, might have a man bun. I can't tell from this angle."

"Are you kidding me? Do you even know me?"

"All right, all right." Jess laughed. "Seven o'clock, corner seat. Baseball cap and beer in hand."

"Baseball hat inside usually means he's hiding something. Probably a comb-over. Next!"

"Gosh damn, you're picky. Okay. Hmm … you okay with a dad bod? I see a lot of those."

"Damn it, Jess. I need to be picked up and put up against the wall. You think a dad bod can do that?"

"You're pretty tiny, so yeah. I mean, what do you weigh? Like, a hundred pounds, soaking wet?"

"Hardly, but thanks." I took a long sip of my drink and winced.

The bartender had been a little too heavy-handed tonight. I wasn't sure if I was going to choke or cry after that first sip. Instead, I just bit my lip like a badass who could handle it and secretly apologized to my liver.

Jess and I were still scouting the room when the band's host stepped up to the stage.

"Before we get the show started tonight, folks, we have a special guest. He usually moonlights down the street at those *other* bars ... but tonight, we're going to show him just how much better *our* bar is. Isn't that right?" the host called out to the cheering crowd. "Are you ready?" he asked the audience.

I looked around and noticed there were a lot of women crowding the stage area.

*Who is this guy anyway? What's so special about him? Unless he has the moves like Jagger, I doubt I'll be entertained.*

"Give it up for ... Jason Jones!" he shouted before exiting the stage. His departure sent even more women scrabbling to the front when they heard who was playing.

"Damn, what's with all these women going nuts?" I asked Jess.

She just shrugged. Apparently, we had been out of the loop too long. That was what happened when you started to get old. Although, at twenty-nine, I didn't think I could be called old ... yet. Maybe next year when I hit that big three-zero. I didn't like to think about that.

I stood up to try to get a better look at the stage as the artist made his way front and center. I didn't have the best eyesight, but even from the back of the room, I could see biceps, biceps, biceps—and some more biceps. Also tattoos. Also ... well, *fuck!* He was my one-night stand—maybe two-nights stand. Hell, this guy I would take every single night of my life if I were given the chance.

I glanced over at Jess and could see her jaw had dropped as well.

*Where are we? Do they really make men like this in Nashville? No way he is from here. That body, those piercing eyes, that tousled hair … damn.*

I tightly squeezed my legs together as I felt myself start to throb.

"I choose him," I whispered to Jess.

Dumbstruck, she nodded and continued staring at the live Roman statue before us.

"Good evening, ladies and gentlemen! Very pleased to be here with you all tonight. I've got a few songs I'm going to sing for y'all tonight before your favorite band graces the stage. Now, some of these songs you might've heard before. Some are old; some are new. Some are happy; some are blue." He winked at the women in front of him.

"But most of all, I just want y'all to have fun tonight. You think you can do that for me?" he said to the crowd of salivating women and curious men. "All right then. You know it, you sing along with me. Deal?"

The crowd hollered and whistled, and someone even made a meow sound from the back.

"All right! Let's get this party started!"

He opened his mouth to sing, and that was when I immediately felt the elastic in my panties melt off. And if they didn't melt all the way off by the time he was done onstage, he could take them off himself— with his teeth. Now, I had never been one for super Southern—aka redneck—accents, but Jason didn't have a redneck accent at all. He had Matthew McConaughey's voice on a Superman body. His face alone was worth writing a song about. In fact, I was sure the love song he was singing was really about his face—not some hot chick, but his own damn face.

"Going in for a closer look!" I told Jess as I grabbed my drink and scurried toward the stage.

She was still staring at Jason, stupefied and in a trance like the rest of the women in here. But I didn't have a lot of time to waste, and by the looks of it, I had a ton of competition. I needed to see and be seen—by him—and ASAP. I had to catch his eye—at least before these other cougars and fangirls did anyway.

I squeezed myself in beside the stage, as close as I could get, squishing in between two doe-eyed sorority girls. I fluttered my lashes and looked up at him, hoping he would look down at me.

*Hey, Mr. Guitar-Strumming, Straight-Up Sex on Those Strings, please look at me! Come get your participation trophy right here. I'm hot and ready!*

"Any requests tonight from this amazing crowd? Don't be shy now. Let's hear it!" He peered out into the dimly lit room.

"I do! I do!" a voice shouted from the back.

*Uh-oh. I know that voice. This can't be good—or can it?*

"It's my BFF's birthday tonight. She's standing right there in front of you. Long and lustrous auburn hair, little black dress, sexy red heels. Yeah, that's her," Jess shouted as she made her way to the front and beside me.

Jason had his head cocked to the side as he listened to Jess, but his eyes stared straight into mine.

He looked like a deer caught in headlights, and I so wanted to crash right into him.

*Wow, he is staring hard. Do I have a really gnarly booger hanging out of my nose or something?* I shifted my feet around, antsy and uncomfortable.

"Well, ya see," Jess continued, "she's just recently gone back on the market. And I think she would love nothing more for her birthday than for you to croon a little song in her ear. How 'bout it?"

"Is that right?" he asked as he started to part his lips in a grin. His dazzling smile sent up long-drawn-out sighs from everyone around me—myself included.

"Liz! Her name is Liz!" Jess said, hopping up and down.

I could feel my cheeks grow hot and my palms start to sweat as all eyes focused on me. I wasn't sure if this could get any worse.

"Come on up here, Liz." He grabbed another barstool from the side of the stage and set it beside him, patting it to beckon me up.

*Shit. Yes, it can get worse.*

I squeezed Jess's arm and gave her the look of murder, to which she just replied with a thumbs-up sign as she pushed me up onto the stage. I was going to have to talk to her about her wingwoman skills.

*This is a recipe for disaster—not for hooking up.*

The crowd murmured as I very carefully tiptoed my way to the barstool beside him. I'd seen one too many YouTube videos of people falling on their ass onstage, and I wasn't going to be the next viral sensation.

*Not today,* echoed in my head.

Jason reached out and took my hand. He looked me dead in the eyes and put his lips to my knuckles. "Pleased to meet you, Liz. Have a seat."

I was sure he could tell I was nervous. The sweat starting to form on my forehead would let everyone know that I was two seconds away from peeing my pants right next to this godlike creature. I was way too afraid to look out into the crowd, so I kept my eyes on him and smiled, completely terrified. I felt his gaze size me up from the tip of my newly highlighted hair to my sexy red heels. He licked his lips.

*Did I just imagine that? No, definitely not. I couldn't have. Maybe he is just thirsty. I should offer him a drink. That was more my style of putting out a feeler. Not this shit Jess had pulled.*

He started to sing John Mayer's "Your Body Is a Wonderland."

*Fuck! There they go. Panties. Done. Burned. Off.*

I didn't even need him to touch me. That had done it.

*I'm done. Got ridden hard. Just hang me out to dry now. I am D-E-A-D.*

But no, he still went on and on and on, singing the most swoonworthy words, as he watched me practically melt into a puddle on the floor.

*Oh my gosh, why is he eye-fucking me like that? This shit is ridiculous. I think I just got pregnant!*

I sat, mesmerized, with the goofiest of grins plastered across my face right up until he hit the last note.

"Happy birthday, Liz. And I mean what I sang; your body is just that." He winked.

I didn't even remember what exactly had happened after that. All I could remember was the crowd cheering and the women giggling. Jess had had to come and pull me off the stage—apparently, after I didn't get the hint that my time to shine was up.

Somehow, I'd ended up back at the bar, and I was on my third negroni before I snapped out of it.

"Dude, are you okay now? Can you talk? Are you pissed off at me?" Jess waved her hands in front of my face.

"No, of course I'm not pissed. I'm fucking livid! What the hell were you thinking?" I said to her. Mostly joking. *Mostly*.

"I'm trying to get you laid! Team Jizz, remember!?"

"I didn't ask for a serenade in front of all of Nashville! Geez Louise!" I tried to sound exasperated, but I couldn't stop smiling.

"Shut up! You liked it!" Jess teased back.

"Yeah, I did." I shrugged. "But all it got me was a ton of embarrassment and a titty hard-on!" I laughed and finished my drink.

Jess's eyes grew wide as she stared right at me.

"What? You've never heard of a titty hard-on?" I asked, confused, because I knew Jess was way kinkier than me. At least, she was for now—until I got my hands on someone willing to experiment a little bit with me.

"Liz—"

"It means, my nipples were hard. I could probably cut glass with them if he sang like that to me again," I rambled on.

"Liz!" Jess smacked my knee and quickly shook her head. Her finger barely lifted to point behind me.

"*Your body is a—*" Jason sang in my ear, sending me tumbling off my chair before he caught me. "I'm so sorry! I didn't mean to scare you!" he quickly apologized. His puppy-dog eyes wouldn't have him in the doghouse for very long—or even at all.

"How much of that conversation did you just hear?" I asked, but his grin already told me the answer to that.

"Just enough to know that I'd like to sing to you again. And again. And maybe again. Definitely again!"

"Great! Nice knowing ya! I'm going to go crawl in a hole now, I think," I stammered as I gathered my things to go.

"No way! Hey! It's your birthday. At least let me buy you a drink."

"You don't need to do that! Your song was enough of an amazing gift! Thanks though. I'm just going"—I looked around for a place to escape—"that way!" I pointed at the exit door. "Come on, Jess. We gotta run!"

Jess giggled and watched our exchange like we were some sort of comedic relief for her. She was having way too much fun with this situation. She sat her butt firmly on her barstool and didn't even attempt to move despite my pleas.

"I think I'm still thirsty, Liz. Aren't you thirsty? You were so thirsty when we came here. So … damn … thirsty." She giggled.

At that moment, I decided that I was not on Team Jizz anymore. I was about to be on Team Fuck Y'all and Bitch Bye!

"Want me to sing something silly for you? Will that help? How about 'C Is for Cookie'? Or a nursery rhyme?" he joked, pulling up a barstool and sitting alongside us. "Come on. Sit down with me, Liz.

Please? I could use some company tonight. Let's toast to your birthday. How old are you anyway?"

"Actually," I started as Jess tried to subtly kick me from under the bar, "it's not even my birthday. This chick right here just likes to get us into trouble." I side-eyed Jess.

"In my defense, I was only trying to be a good wingwoman! I mean, if she were put front and center, in the spotlight, and I just so happened to mention that she was on the market, then every man in here could get a good look at her, right? I mean, look at her! She's the jackpot!"

"Jess!" I grew even more uncomfortable.

She was going to get an earful as soon as this sexpot next to me left. I felt the steam from his hotness start to cloud my brain and make me fuzzy, or that could be the alcohol—probably a little bit of both.

"She's right. You *are* the jackpot. Wonderland and all. But about this fake birthday … I guess that means no birthday spankings then, huh?" He frowned, making his heart-stopping puppy eyes.

Jess nearly choked on her drink. "I'm all right. I'm all right! Just gonna run to the ladies' room real quick. See ya!" She scurried away, turning around only long enough to give me a quick wink and thumbs-up before she disappeared, leaving me—and Jason—all alone.

"Now, I didn't say I was opposed to spankings, but …" I took a deep breath and grabbed at my chance. I had come here for one reason tonight—for him. I just hadn't known it until I saw him walk on that stage like he'd just come down from Mount

Olympus. Now that he was here, in front of me, well …

*I gotta do what I gotta do.*

And Jason was what I had to do.

"Mmhmm." He leaned over to whisper in my ear, "How bad do you want it?"

His breath tickled my neck, sending every single hair on my body standing at attention. His attention.

*Sir, yes, sir.*

"Check, please!" I called. My heart raced. I could feel the blood pump through my cheeks, my titty hard-ons, my inner thighs. I had never done anything like this before. Okay, that was a lie. I had—but not with someone like *him*.

"I got it." He winked as he pulled out his wallet. "After all, it's your pretend birthday, right?"

*Best pretend birthday ever.*

"Where are we going? I need to text Jess real quick and let her know."

"We aren't leaving. I've got a changing room in the back. Come check it out," he said as he grabbed my hand and pulled me up.

I quickly texted Jess while he led me through the crowd.

> *Me: Be back soon. Give me an hour? Maybe two. ;)*

> *Jess: You're not going home with him, are you?*

> *Me: No! Just headed to the changing room in the back. Be back shortly. Promise.*

*Jess: Fine! But I get juicy details. I'll be back at the bar. Same place you abandoned me at.*

*Me: Ha! You left me! And besides, this was your idea. Thankfully.*

*Jess: You're right. Enjoy it. Lucky girl! No cheesy tacos either. You'd better rubber that ducky.*

*Me: Lucky ducky.*

*Jess: Sucky, sucky!*

"What are you giggling about?" Jason asked, opening the door to the changing room.

It was so dimly lit that I could barely see anything, and he didn't even attempt to turn on a light.

*Does he not want to see what he is doing with me? Is something wrong? Is he not attracted to me? Am I a butterface?*

"Oh, nothing! I was just telling Jess I would meet her back at the bar afterward, is all," I replied as I let my eyes adjust to my surroundings—mirror, chair, couch, closet. Nothing special. It looked like a stereotypical changing room. Not that I'd ever been in a changing room, but I had seen plenty on TV. That counted, right?

"Uh-huh. You two seem like trouble," he said as he took my hand and led me to the couch.

It looked clean enough, but the nurse in me wanted to sanitize the hell out of it.

*People have probably been banging on this couch for years. Yuck.*

I forced that dirty thought out of my mind and focused on dirty thoughts with the rock star in front of me.

"We're the good kind of trouble." I grinned. I was even more nervous now.

*How long has it been since I had nooky? Weeks? Months? Years?*

Jason took a step toward me, licking his lips as if he wanted to eat me alive. I couldn't even think straight when he looked at me like that.

"So, you're a bad girl?" he asked.

His hand reached out, and he slowly traced the back of his index finger down from my shoulder to my palm, circling it until I clenched it in my fist and pulled him into me.

"I can be your bad girl," I whispered as he leaned down to kiss me.

His hand rested on the back of my head as he gently pushed me toward his mouth. His tongue slipped over mine, warm and wet. Just like me.

"I think you're a very good girl," he said, pulling back. "So good that you're going to do as I say. Are you okay with that?"

*Uh, what?* I wasn't so sure I knew how to answer that.

*Is this going to get weird? Or bad? Or creepy? I do want to try non-vanilla sex, but what exactly does he have in mind? Maybe I need to sign some kind of contract ...*

He cautiously stepped back. He must have seen the hesitation in my face.

"I'm sorry. I didn't mean it in a creepy way. I just meant, if you want to try something a little rough and kinky. I only have your best interests in mind. I'll not hurt you. But I understand if you want to just, ya know, do it. Or not. We don't have to do anything. Up to the birthday girl."

*Well, this is what I came here for, right? Something not so ho-hum. And with him—Jason Jones? Easy choice. I wonder what he has in mind.*

"Let's do it." I smiled as my heart beat out of my chest. Thankfully, I knew the signs of cardiac arrest.

"That's, *Yes, please, Mr. Jones,*" he said as he grabbed a condom from a nearby drawer.

*Oh, hell yes.*

"Yes, please, Mr. Jones," I moaned as he pulled me into him.

His hands stealthily slipped up my thighs and removed my panties before I even had time to get my head in the game—his game. I instinctively grabbed for him. My hands reached for the bulge in his pants as he removed his belt.

*Damn, it's a nice bulge. A very nice, hard, thick bulge.* I felt it pulsing in my palm.

"You are a naughty girl! I'm going to have to tie those hands up," he said as he turned me around and very loosely tied my hands behind my back with his belt.

He sat on the edge of the couch and steered me backward, toward him. I wasn't sure what to do with myself anymore. I just let him have control—which was so not like me, but this was hot as fuck!

"Birthday spankings for the bad girl," he said as he motioned for me to lie across his lap. Facedown, ass up.

Normally, I would feel pretty damn vulnerable in this position, but with Jason, I was way too hot and bothered to resist.

"Let me see that perfect little ass of yours." His hands glided all the way up the backs of my thighs and lifted my dress up until my bare butt was right in his face. "Damn, Liz. You have the perfect round ass. Like a peach I want to bite."

He leaned down to bite my left ass cheek while he gave my right one a hard slap. I moaned as I felt an electric tingle shoot all the way down to between my legs.

"How many birthday spankings is it?"

"Twenty-nine," I whispered. I could barely get the words out. I was breathless already, and we were just getting started.

*I should have told him fifty.*

"One … two …" he counted out as he slapped my ass hard, smoothing his hand over my cheeks and gently caressing them after each slap. "Are you wet enough for me yet?" He slid his finger between my legs and slowly moved it in and out. "Almost. But I think I can make you drip for me."

He slipped another finger inside and another. He pushed them in as deep as he could until I squirmed. I needed to feel him inside me.

"Oh, good girl. Such a good girl. You're so fucking wet. But you still need more spankings. You've been bad, very bad with your pretend birthday. I think you'll need extra punishment for that," he growled and continued to slap my ass.

I had the full twenty-nine spankings and then some. By the time he was done, I was ravenous.

"Mmm … I like that." He dipped his fingers into me again and found out just how turned on he had made me. He thrust them into me harder and then gently. Back and forth, back and forth until my hips dug into his thighs and my legs started to twitch uncontrollably.

"Are you ready for me, Liz?" he asked as he kept working his fingers inside me. His other hand rubbed the stinging tingle that still lingered on my ass cheeks.

"Yes, please, *Mr. Jones.*" I bit my lip and practically bucked on his lap. I had been ready for this before I even left my house.

"Good girl."

He pulled me to my feet and bent me over the couch, on my knees. My hands were still tied behind my back. I could hear him rip the condom open behind me while his pants hit the floor. I braced myself, remembering just how thick his bulge was in my hand.

*Oh fuck, oh fuck, oh fuck.*

I felt his hands on my hips first. His fingertips dug into my flesh as he grabbed me hard and pulled me back and straight into his cock. I gasped as he slid right inside me, stretching me out.

*Whoa.*

My eyes crossed. Thankfully, I was turned around, and he couldn't see the goofy look that spread across my face.

"Oh damn," I said as my body trembled.

His hands left my hips as he reached for my hair, gathered it in his fist, and pulled it tightly. His other hand reached around to find my clit as he drove himself into me hard.

"I want you to come for me, Liz. But not until I say you can, okay? Otherwise, more spankings."

I could only nod and whimper, as I was already holding myself back.

"That's my girl."

He slammed into me harder. My hair was still wrapped around his wrist as he turned my neck, so I could watch him. His lip parted in little grunts each time he slowly dived into me.

"Look at me. Don't you close your eyes. Look straight into mine. I want you to come for me. Don't look away, or we'll stop and start all over." His hand smacked my ass hard again, making me gasp.

*Really? Is that the worst punishment he can think of?*

I wished I could start a million times over, but this right now was just too fucking good to stop.

He reached around to flicker his fingers against my clit. I made sure my eyes didn't leave his even though my eyes felt like they were about to roll into the back of my head.

I wouldn't dare disobey Mr. Jones. *Hell no.* Not right now anyway. Not while he was doing the thing … all the things … and doing them oh-so damn well.

I started to moan louder. I could feel myself begin to lose control. My hips pushed back into him, rolling against his fingers, his cock. He sensed I was close, and he drove himself into me even deeper. I cried out as he growled behind me.

"That's it, my sweet girl. Come for me. Let me feel that pussy of yours throb on my dick. I'm going to make *you* sing for *me* this time."

And … I lost it. I didn't think I had ever moaned so loud in my life. I could probably be heard over the band outside. I might as well have been singing opera. I hit high notes I hadn't even known I had in me. I was going to walk out of this room, and everyone would clap in a standing ovation for the howling woman in the back.

"Fuck," he said as my body spasmed around him. His cock jumped inside of me with one last deep push before he collapsed into me, and I collapsed into the couch.

We caught our breath as we both grew as limp as dishrags.

"Happy pretend birthday, Liz." He kissed the back of my neck and untied my hands.

"Thanks, Mr. Jones." I giggled, still breathing heavy. My knees trembled as I tried to stand up and wobbled, falling back down to the couch.

"Let me help you." He laughed as he pulled me up and held me steady. "You okay?"

"More than okay," I said, getting ahold of myself. "I needed that."

"So did I! You're amazing, Liz. So damn amazing," he said as he knelt down and helped me slip my panties back on.

My hands steadied myself on his shoulders, so I wouldn't tip over again. I watched him get dressed, thinking of how I'd just lived the fantasy of probably every woman who had been in this bar tonight.

"Come on, my little limp noodle. Let's get you back to your friend." He offered his arm to me.

"I think if I tried, I could probably float out of here," I replied.

Our giggles were lost in the noise around us as we opened the door and headed back out toward the bar.

The look on Jess's face as she saw us walk back was priceless. A mixture of amusement, shock, curiosity, and pride danced across her mischievous smile.

"Well, thanks for bringing her back in one piece, Jason!" she said as she elbowed me and smiled. "You ready to go? Luke will be here in a minute."

I noticed a look of confusion cross Jason's face.

"Her husband, Luke, picks us up, so we don't have to Uber. He likes to make sure we're safe."

"Sounds like a perfect gentleman. And a lucky man to have you two to entertain him, I'm sure."

"You've no idea!" Jess laughed.

If Jason had any idea, he would probably run the other way.

"The best kind of trouble, right?" Jason grinned and pulled out his phone. "I would love to get in trouble with you again, Liz, if you would like that? You know, for your real birthday shenanigans or just a regular Tuesday night. Whatever."

*How can I resist that smile? That voice? Those biceps? That cock?*

"Should I store your number under Mr. Jones then?" I teased.

Jess watched us exchange numbers, eyebrows raised so high that she would need Botox for a year.

"Such a good girl." He leaned down to kiss my forehead.

A forehead kiss—that wasn't just a one-night stand kind of thing. That was a boyfriend-girlfriend type of thing.

*What is he thinking? Did he not get the memo? We just had hot sex. Only hot sex! He can't go doing romantic stuff like that! That would lead way to the feels … yikes!*

I couldn't have that. I promised myself no feels until I hit thirty—at least. But that was a year away—or actually less. I didn't like to think about my biological clock ticking. It stressed me out.

"Come on, good girl. We gotta get going." Jess pulled at my arm and led me out of there.

I knew she was ready to hear all about it.

I said a quick good-bye and followed her out the door. I could feel his eyes still on me as I hobbled away.

*Am I walking funny?* I hated it when people watched me walk away. It made my legs not work properly.

I still felt a tremble in my knee and a throb in my panties as I unintentionally sashayed out the door.

## JASON

I could feel my cock jump with every bounce in her step as I watched Liz walk away. That sweet ass swung from side to side. I wondered if she still had my palm imprint on it. She had taken me in like a champ and played along with my little game. I hadn't done anything like that in so long. But something had told me Liz could handle it—and handle me.

*And handle it she did.* I grinned.

I sighed as I waited on my erection to go down so that I could stand up. I saw the other women linger around me, waiting to see if they would be the one I chose to bring home tonight. But not only was I already spent, but I also wasn't interested. Surprisingly, I didn't sleep with every woman I met. Liz had just felt different, and she was so damn hot.

She was hotter than anyone in here by far. I glanced around at the hopefuls, finished my drink, tabbed out, and headed toward the door—alone. I was completely satisfied tonight. There wouldn't be a round two.

*Unless Liz …*

I paused and thought about texting her before I headed home. *Nah.* She was probably getting ready for bed, and I had to go home to Deuce.

And by Deuce, I meant my dog, not the other thing. He was my shithead dog, properly named Deuce. He was the reason I couldn't bring women back to my house. He was a mixture of ugly and butt ugly with a side of leg-humper and farty. He'd also chewed a hole in my rug, my couch, and my bed frame. None of which I cared enough to replace … yet. Who was I trying to impress anyway? If the right woman came along, sure. But I had just gotten back into the game, and I had no plans to settle down anytime soon.

As I drove the trek back home, my mind wandered to what she would be like—the right woman. I thought I'd had all that before, but it had vanished, just like the streetlights that suddenly stopped right before my long gravel driveway.

*Poof. Just like that.* One minute, everything was bright, and you could see where you were going, and the next minute, someone turned out the lights, and you wondered where you were and what you were heading toward.

I knew this drive like the back of my hand. But my personal life? As in women? The lights were still out, and I was as confused as ever.

Usually, that confusion translated well on paper— in song form. And luckily for me, people actually liked it—and by people, I meant women. Some of them were hot, and some of them filled me with the type of anxiousness someone could only get when they heard the banjos playing out in the middle of nowhere. But most of my fans were cute. I would admit, the attention was nice. I didn't have to be alone every night if I didn't want to be alone. It was just my choice to be alone—for now, or at least until I got myself back together. I wondered if I would ever get my head sorted out and if anyone ever actually had their head sorted out. My deep musings on that quiet drive took me all the way back home and into the door where a very impatient Deuce waited on me.

"Come on, Deuce," I said as I made my way to the fridge and cracked open a beer, heading toward the patio.

Deuce growled with impatience, demanding that I stop to give him attention. I rolled my eyes and leaned down to scratch behind his ear. Once he settled, he was actually great company, especially on nights like this—those nights when I wasn't yet ready to go to sleep or be alone with my thoughts in that big, empty bed of mine. Deuce always kept me entertained even if he was a demanding little shit.

My patio was my pride and joy—my man cave. It was always a quiet and calming place, the perfect spot to think. The crickets chirped, the wind rustled in the trees, the smell of charred meats wafted up from my grill. Whenever I came out here I always felt like I needed to howl at the moon, like some type of caveman. If I ever needed to clear my mind to do some thinking, working, songwriting, or drinking, it was here.

I had no neighbors nearby for at least twenty acres. I could piss in my own backyard or fiddle my diddle outside anytime I pleased without being worried that someone was watching me. Not that I did any of that out here in the open, but I could if I wanted to. I just didn't want to because … well, that would be creepy as fuck. But my private patio was useful for making love under the stars and getting so loud that you might think you'd wake the neighbors, but you wouldn't. They didn't exist. It had been a while since I did that too.

I wondered if Liz would like me to spank her ass out here. All goose bumps and tingles on her blushing flesh. Our primal moans would get loud enough to scare the birds out of the trees. I felt my cock jump in my pants as I stared at my phone and contemplated on texting her to make sure she had made it home all right. Of course I was sure she had made it home just fine. She'd looked like she was in good hands. But I wanted her in *my* hands—again. I shook the thought out of my head. It was too late. I should get myself to bed now anyhow.

*Stupid early morning shift at the coffee shop and all,* I groaned.

My eyes grew heavy as I finished my beer and stood up to head toward my bed with Deuce waddling his fat butt behind me.

"Late night, huh, there, Jason?" my boss, Brad, asked when he saw me crawl into work a few days later.

"Oh, ya know, the usual. Late-night gigs. Gotta pay the bills!" I replied, half-teasing but mostly serious. This job didn't pay shit.

Brad laughed like he knew what I was talking about. He had been born into money and had it ever since. He owned the coffee shop among a hundred other investments. He loved to let everyone know about them all as he sat on his laptop in the corner, groaning and gloating about his stocks and barking orders at any employee in his line of sight. Brad was the kind of guy you wanted to punch in the face—with a rusty barstool.

*That would be a great line in my next song,* I mused.

"Maybe you can pick up an extra shift or two this week. Cut back on all that croonin' onstage. Those are pipe dreams. Won't get you nowhere. Especially in this town. You know how hard it is to make it in Music City? Everyone and their moms out there, singing on the street corners," Brad said, shaking his head.

I imagined him shaking it so hard that it fell off and rolled under the table, and that was the end of Brad.

"Yeah? Well, what if I'm not trying to get anywhere with my singing? What if that's not the point?"

Brad looked up at me as if I'd spouted blasphemy. The only language he knew was money.

"What do you mean, you don't want to get anywhere? You mean, you can be perfectly happy at an entry-level job and playing around onstage at night? You said you gotta pay the bills. Lord knows this job won't do it!"

*Yeah, ya damn dipshit. Maybe you should pay your employees an actual living wage.*

I held my tongue. I didn't exactly need this job right now, but the extra money was nice, and the experience in running a coffee shop I needed.

"I didn't say I would be happy at an entry-level job my entire life. And what I do with my guitar is hardly playing. I'm just saying, for now, I'm happy. I'm surrounded by beautiful women, booze, and good tunes almost every night. What's not to love?" I shrugged.

I knew that would hit him in his soft spot—his soft, bald spot. Brad never made it with the ladies. Not any ladies … or men … that I'd been aware of. It was obvious why. He was an asshole—and not one of those alpha assholes the ladies seemed to love these days either. This dude had nothing going for him, except his finances. And even that hefty bank account of his couldn't help his asshole personality. People still cringed and ran the other direction once he opened his mouth. He was just a regular old turd muffin.

"It's almost rush time. A little less talk, a lot more action," Brad sneered. His lips were pursed so tight; it looked like he talked out of his asshole—which he usually did because he was all asshole.

I turned back around just as the crowd started to gather. Yep, Brad was someone I wanted to punch in the face. But lately, I'd been doing one better. I had always wanted to open a coffee shop with live music, so when the opportunity had fallen into my lap, I had taken it. I'd purchased the property a while ago, and I had been sitting on it, trying to figure out my next move.

*What will you think about that, Brad?*

I smiled as I continued making drinks. My mind drifted to my rendezvous with Liz a few nights before. I hadn't even had the balls to call her yet. I wasn't sure what to say and how exactly this dating thing worked anymore.

*How ya doing? Ready for round two? Still got my fingerprints on that sweet ass of yours? Want to go on a date or skip straight to bed?*

I rolled the thoughts of her wet pussy and slick thighs around in my head while I made customer's drink orders. It certainly helped pass the time.

"What are you smiling about over there, Jason?" My coworker, Rob, grinned.

Rob sometimes showed up at my gigs to pick up ladies. He always came in the next day with a dirty story to tell.

"I was grinning? Hell if I know!" I shrugged, still lost in thoughts of Liz and how I'd had my hands tangled in her hair as she moaned one of the most primal moans I'd ever heard. *Damn, that was so fucking hot.*

"Ahh!" I cried out after I stupidly let the steam out of the kettle and up and straight onto my arm.

Thinking about sex while working in a kitchen should be like drinking and driving—dangerous as hell and a big no-no.

"Oh my gosh! That looks terrible!" Rob grimaced. A look of disgust shadowed his face as he stared wide-eyed at my arm that was turning redder and redder by the second.

"What now? What happened? Am I going to have to pay workers' comp? What did you do?" Brad waddled over with his hands on his hips like the authority figure he thought he was. One sight of my arm, and he turned around and waved me off. "Go. Now. I'll find someone to cover your shift." He rolled his eyes.

"Hey, man, are you going to be okay? Want me to ask if I can have some time off to drive you to the ER?" Rob said, breathing heavy with his mouth hung open.

I thought for sure he was going to pass out if he kept looking at it.

"It's not like I'm dying! I might feel like it, but I'm not! Yeah, I think I'll be okay. I can drive. I'm out. Try not to let the incel in the corner fuck your day up," I squeaked out, the pain making my voice shake.

Rob laughed and clapped me on the back. I didn't like to ask for help, and even though I had no idea how I was going to drive, the searing pain slicing through my arm kept me moving forward. I would have walked to the damn ER if I had to. My jaw clenched as I ran to my car, so I could scream out in pain.

I barely made it to the hospital while I drove with my left arm—the good one. At this point, my right arm didn't want to move—or I didn't want to move it … or I couldn't move it. Even without moving it, it felt like a thousand needles were stabbing every inch of my skin. I felt the sweat run down my forehead as I entered the hospital. Luckily, there were only two others waiting in line in front of me, which meant I would probably be waiting for only a few hours.

*'Murica.*

I sat down in the waiting area, closed my eyes, and focused on something, anything, other than this hot pile of scorched skin that used to be my arm. To my surprise, the triage nurse almost immediately called me back and put me in a makeshift room. I waited for what felt like an eternity and wondered if this was what hell was like.

*A little more church, a little less drinking,* I promised myself.

The curtain finally pulled back, and both of us jumped with shock. Liz stood before me, still as beautiful as ever, even in her plain-Jane scrubs instead of that tight, little black dress she had worn only a few nights before. Her fiery-red hair was pulled up in a ponytail—a ponytail I would love to yank on while I slammed into her from behind.

"Oh! Hey! Well, this is awkward," she said, biting her lip.

I had the feeling that she wished she'd looked at my chart before stepping inside this little room.

"What brings you in today, *Mr. Jones?*" She cut right to the chase. *Professional and curt.* But she wore a sly smile as soon as she called me by my last name.

My cock stirred in my pants as I felt myself getting turned on already.

"A nurse? I would have thought you were more suited to taking orders instead of giving them." I held my arm up, so she could see the damage.

"Oh, Mr. Jones ... if you only knew." She gently grabbed my arm and inspected it. "This is pretty terrible actually. At least the burn missed your tattoos though! How did you do this anyway?"

"Steam." I cringed as she turned my arm from side to side. "I work at a café in The Gulch. I wasn't focused and made a dumb mistake." My palms started to sweat. I didn't know if it was from the uncomfortable situation or the fact that my skin felt as if it were melting off my elbow.

"Oh. So, not only are you a famous musician, but you are also a coffee connoisseur? That's interesting. What else don't I know about you?" she asked as she picked up my file. "Kidding. I'm kidding! You know I'm actually just checking for allergies—and maybe your age. I have a bet going with Jess." Her big blue eyes quickly scanned the pages.

*Oh no*, I thought. *Oh God.*

That file hadn't been updated since I was here five years ago for a minor car accident. I knew what was in that file. I would have rather have had a bad case of hemorrhoids in that file than what she was about to see.

I watched her, waiting and knowing just how this was about to play out. I broke out in an even sweatier sweat, if that was possible. And ... there it was. Her lips went from a wide grin to *I'm about to cut this asshole* in a quick minute. Second even. Millisecond.

"So, no allergies. That's good. I'll get something started for you, and the doctor will be in shortly," she said without a trace of the spunky, fun, pep-in-the-step Liz who had walked in here a minute ago.

"Do I need to—" I started, wondering if I needed to keep my arm elevated. I thought I'd heard that somewhere. I really had no idea what I was doing. I had never been burned before. Not like this anyhow. My burns were usually in the form of old flames.

*Yet another good lyric for a song.*

"You do nothing," she cut me off. The look in her eyes was so deadly that I even felt my asshole clench tight. "I'll alert the doctor and get you taken care of. Anything else, Jason?"

"No, I guess not. Hey, are you okay?"

"Have a good day then." She left, tossing the curtain behind her as if she'd tossed her flame-red hair in a final *fuck off* flip.

I sat on the edge of the hospital bed, alone and in pain. I'd hurt Liz and not even meant to. The change in her expression when she'd read my file was depressing. I liked Liz. She hadn't been just a fun romp in the hay. The truth was, she'd been stuck in my head since I took her hand and led her onstage that night. From what little I knew about her, so far, she'd been a really cool chick. At least, that was the vibe I'd gotten before she picked up my chart. I was going to have to explain to her and apologize about that when she came back. It wasn't like I had done anything wrong. Not exactly anyway. It was a tough situation and one that I hadn't even asked to be in.

I waited for what seemed like hours. My mind tossed and turned, offering up different explanations. I decided on being truthful even though I didn't like to speak about the truth. It was more shameful than any story I could come up with. I let my thoughts drift to the patients around me. I could hear Liz bark off instructions to the crotchety old man beside me. To be fair, he deserved her wrath, which I thought I had been the cause of. Actually, I knew I had been the cause of it. But his constant whining and rudeness hadn't helped *his* cause out any.

Apparently, he had a wild case of poison ivy that covered half his body. Too bad it wasn't in his mouth, so he could keep it shut. If he kept talking to her like that, I was likely going to open the curtain myself and give him a knuckle sandwich to fill that loud mouth of his. But not to my surprise, Liz handled him. I thought she could handle anyone who came at her. Even I'd been getting a little anxious for what she would do to me once she came back inside my hidey-hole. I waited and waited and waited on her return.

"Jason Jones, star of Music Row, isn't that right?" the doctor said as she pulled the curtain back.

"I wouldn't exactly say star …" I stammered, looking up at her as she stared down at me.

Her eyes pierced right through mine. She knew.

"Not from what I've heard around here. Seems you got a name for yourself, *Jason*," she said while she checked my chart, only pausing briefly to look over at my arm and back to the chart again. "It's pretty bad, but you'll live. I can give you something for the pain, but you'll have to stay here awhile if you take it."

She cocked her head to the side. She knew I wanted to be out of here—and fast. I was uncomfortable on so many damn levels.

"I'm good. Like you said, I'll live." I cringed. The pain was only slightly better since getting here, but I could handle physical pain much more than this emotional drama I was enduring.

*I have to tell Liz the truth.*

"Thought so. I'll write you a prescription for some ointment and also for the pain, so you can at least get some sleep tonight. The nurse will put your dressing on and show you how to change it. Just keep on top of it, and everything will be fine. If you notice any swelling or fever or if your pain gets worse, get back in here. Got it?"

"Yes, ma'am." I nodded. *Maybe I should have taken something for the pain if Liz will be wrapping my arm.*

She liked to play rough, and at this point, I could only imagine how rough she wanted to be with me. I felt the panic arising in me as I waited and got my story in order.

"Mr. Jones?" an unfamiliar voice called out. It wasn't Liz. "I'll be taking care of your arm today and getting you back out of here and on your way."

"Okay. Thanks. Is my nurse, Liz, not coming back in? I was hoping to ask her some questions."

"I'll be your nurse now. Liz is swamped with other patients at the moment. I told her I would help her out. We cover for each other like that. It's kind of a sisterhood thing we have in this department. Being there for each other and all. Sharing stories … drama … but anyway, feel free to ask me anything. I can help."

So, she knew too. *Sisterhood.* I had fallen right into the lion's den. If Liz was going to avoid me, then I'd just have to text her and explain things.

"It's fine. Nothing important," I said as she began to slather salve on my arm. I thought I had seen a hint of a smirk on her face each time I winced.

Back at home and safely on my patio, I caught everyone up on today's events. Luckily, I didn't have another gig until this weekend. I should be okay by then. I had to be anyway. Predictably, Brad was less than understanding when I told him I needed tomorrow off from the café. It was the doctor's orders. Not really, but the thought of using my arm on the morning coffee rush sent a searing pain up my elbow. He insisted that I go back through safety training first thing as soon as I was back. I wished I could tell him that wasn't what I needed. All I needed was to not think about banging hot chicks while I made coffee, and I would be A-okay. I was sure that would go over really well.

I settled into my chair as Deuce ran around the backyard, trying to catch flies, butterflies, and even bees—that wasn't smart, but then again, that was Deuce. I watched his hilarious efforts as I stalled and put off the only other conversation I needed to catch up on. I had to prepare myself for Liz. Something told me she wasn't the type to put up with some shit, and today, I'd handed her a load of it—on a silver platter.

> Me: *Hey. I missed telling you good-bye at the hospital. I had hoped to see you again before I left.*

> Me: *Are you up for a call? I would like to talk to you about earlier today.*

I sent my texts after I retyped it about eighty-two times. I sat and waited and waited, like a desperate son of a bitch. I occupied myself by throwing the Frisbee to Deuce. I watched him crash his nose into the grass, trying to catch it. He wasn't the brightest dog; that was for sure.

I checked my phone, but she still hadn't answered.

*Yet another idea for a song,* I thought as I grabbed my pen and paper. *Guy fucks up, tries to contact girl, but she's moved on? Typical. Except I didn't actually fuck up, did I?*

After two hours or so of eating my frustration in chips and salsa, writing my feelings on paper, strumming my pain through my guitar, and damn near checking my phone every minute, I gave up and headed inside.

Liz was one sweet peach I wouldn't be getting a taste of anymore.

I let out an exasperated sigh and climbed into bed early.

Just when my life had started to pick back up, some shit happened.

My burn throbbed as I slathered more ointment on it. I took a pain pill in desperation, knowing I would be tossing and turning all night with this searing pain that seemed to come and go in waves, both mentally and physically. I tossed the medicine back, swallowed, and put the bottle back in the cabinet. And there it was, staring back at me. That symbol of life until death do us part—my wedding ring. It sat right there, on the edge of the cabinet, right where I had finally taken it off and left it only a few short months ago. My stomach churned, my heart lurched, and my head swam.

I checked my phone one last time. Still no response from Liz. I couldn't blame her.

*3*

## LIZ

My boss had known there was something going on as soon as I walked out of Jason's room and she saw my expression. I tended to wear my heart on my sleeve, so I hadn't ever had any hope in a career as a high-rolling poker badass—or as a regular woman masking her emotions over a Jerky McJerkface. She knew about Mr. Jones, thanks to my coworker Miranda, and Miranda knew about Mr. Jones, thanks to my other coworker Susan. Actually, all of that was a lie. We were a close bunch, and I'd spilled the beans—or I'd not spilled the beans as much as I'd totally bragged and gushed about the rendezvous with Broadway's best, Jason Jones. But I'd only told that to my coworkers—*not* my boss even though she found out anyway and gave me a fist bump.

Our small all-female group of women that work this shift had always been like family. We'd been together for years—through births, deaths, breakups, divorce, and everything in between. Thankfully, we all got along really well, and not once had there ever been any cat fights. These women were a part of my life, and I didn't know what I'd do without them for support, especially at this moment.

After I left Jason's room, all I wanted to do was crawl in a hole, and Dr. Bailey, my boss, immediately picked up on my mood and let me.

"Go take a breather. Miranda will cover your patients. Can I do anything for you? Want me to slap his arm around a bit?" Dr. Bailey grinned. "You know I'm only halfway kidding, right?"

"I know you are." I tried to laugh but settled on an angsty grunt. "No, I'll be fine. Let's just get him out of here. I think I'll take that break though. Just for a few. Let me check the patient next to him and get him settled, and then I'll head down to the cafeteria. I could use a strong coffee."

"I'll have Miranda and the girls cover for you and text you when he checks out. So sorry, Liz." She patted my back.

I checked on my patients, aware that Jason was probably listening to my every word when I was nearby his room. He could probably feel the tension that radiated off of me, searched him out, and punched him in the gut.

*Good.*

I hoped he knew that any future spankings were off the table now—but ass-kickings were still on. And if he didn't know that, he would know soon enough. I would just block and disappear because that had never failed me. It was just easier that way for me unless I wanted to go into full bitch mode and really let him have it, which I was capable of too.

*Decisions, decisions*, I thought as I snuck away to let myself breathe and text Jess.

> *Me: Wanna grab dinner tonight? I could use an ear. It's an E-M-E-R-G-E-N-C-Y.*

My heart had been pounding steadily in my chest ever since I saw he had his wife listed as his emergency contact. I'd double-checked his chart, not trusting my eyes, and sure enough, he was married.

I had seen guilt written across his face as soon as I looked up from his file. I wondered how he got away with all his flirting *and* apparently all his fucking. I was so upset that I couldn't even think straight. I was almost tempted to look the poor lady up on social media and confess our sins, but I needed Jess first. If anyone could talk me down, it would be her.

> *Jess: You okay?*

> *Me: Yeah. Just a long day, and I need to talk. It's about our friend, the singer.*

> *Jess: Yeah, so Mr. Jones called? :)*

> *Me: Not really. I'll have to tell you all about it. Craft cocktails and charcuterie as soon as I get off work?*

> *Jess: You know it! Rooftop, as usual?*

> *Me: Will be there.*

I had so many questions.

*Maybe they are swingers? Maybe he is separated? Maybe he's just an asshole? Why do I always attract assholes anyway? No, better not answer that.*

Whatever it was that Jason and I had shared, that was the end of that—no more spankings and no more Mr. Jones. That was a shame because I'd really liked this new kink thing we had going, and I'd been sure he would contact me soon for round two. The way he'd handled me, he could've told me to lick his boot, and I would have melted. Okay, not really. Nurse … germs … but I would have licked his balls, no problem. He was just that hot. But now, he was just another hot asshole.

I shook the thoughts of him out of my head. My patients had been wearing me out, and I needed to focus—at least until six anyway. I pulled out my phone and checked the time, prolonging my break. I sat back to rest my feet when there it was—a text from Jason. The chicken was coming home to roost—or something like that.

> *Jason: Hey. I missed telling you good-bye at the hospital. I had hoped to see you again before I left.*

> *Jason: Are you up for a call? I would like to talk to you about earlier today.*

*Ha! Up for a call? You've got to be shitting me!*

But I wanted that call. I wanted to know why he hadn't told me he was married, and I wanted to let him have it. By *it*, I meant the sheer force of my ice-queen, super-bitch wrath.

I put my phone down, fuming. I hadn't even known him very long, and he already drove me nuts.

I sighed and decided to get back to work. I hoped my patients would take my mind back off of him. Only two hours to go, and then Team Jizz would tackle this predicament together. But first, I had to tackle my patients, then the infamous Nashville traffic, and then a cocktail—or three.

"Okay, what's this emergency all about?" Jess pulled a chair up to the table.

She was late, as usual. Lucky for her, she had an awesome friend who had already ordered a drink for her, and lucky for me, the waiter had made it easy because he already knew our order as soon as he saw me. We might come here a bit too much.

"Mr. Jones came into the ER today," I said as I twirled my cocktail straw around in my drink and looked out over the city.

The music blared from all angles, drowning out the traffic below. The rooftop hotel bar was our secret hideaway that had become immensely popular and not-so-secret anymore. The food was great, the drinks were great, the music was great, and most of the time, the men looked great too. Business professionals in their suits, musicians in their boots, hipsters in their man buns.

"Oh shit! Is he okay?" Jess's brows furrowed as she clutched her heart.

She was way too emotional for a job in the healthcare industry. That, and the fact that she felt weak at the sight of blood pretty much confirmed that she wouldn't make it as a doctor or a nurse. She preferred to work in an office, doing boss-lady stuff—whatever that was. She mumbled on about deadlines, projects, conference calls, and meetings whenever I asked her. It was almost foreign to me, just as my job at the hospital was to her.

"Oh, he's just dandy! He's sexy, he's funny, he's got a talent for singing, and … he's married!" I added with a big fake smile across my face. I was pretty sure I had psycho eyes at the moment.

"What. The. Fuck? Seriously? How did you find out? Wait!" Jess called the waiter over to tell him to keep them coming as soon as we finished the first drink. "Okay, now, go on. I need to know everything. Guess it wasn't you being naughty after all. Maybe it was him who deserved the spankings?"

"An ass-kicking is more like it," I replied, tossing back my drink as I sat back to tell her everything.

Her mouth hung open as she soaked up all the details so that she could fill her husband in later. I didn't mind how much she shared with him. He usually offered valuable insight from the male perspective but only when asked because … mansplain. He'd been smart enough not to do that—yet.

"So, wait. You haven't responded to his text yet?"

"No. Do you think I should?"

"Super proud of you for holding it in this long, but yeah, I think you should."

"I don't even know what to say. I want to tell him *fuck you*! But I also want to ask him to *fuck me*!"

"Well, shit, that's the cocktails talking. Remember, he is an asshole. A married asshole." She reached across the table to grab my hand and let me down gently.

"You're right. No more Mr. Jones. I wonder what his wife looks like." I hiccuped.

"Oh my gosh, Liz. This isn't a road you want to go down. Just call him and listen to his lame excuses first and then let him know you aren't that type of woman. Then, it's done and over with, and we can toast to finding someone else who spanks that ass and is actually available." She smiled and lifted her glass in salute.

*Team Jizz!*

"Maybe I should put out an ad on the internet. *Looking for spankings, dirty nurse*," I teased.

"If you want to get killed! Now, call him. See what he has to say for himself, so we can laugh at how stupid men can be."

"You don't think it's too late?" I said, checking the time.

It was only nine thirty. Surely, a playboy like him couldn't be asleep by now.

"No. Quit stalling." She wagged her finger at me.

She was right. I was stalling.

I took a few deep breaths and gathered my slightly tipsy thoughts. I could feel the familiar rumblings of nervousness in my stomach. *Or is that the sausage I just ate? Maybe I should head to the restroom before this call?*

"I'm waiting." Jess leaned back into her chair and crossed her arms.

"Fine, fine, fine. I'll call." I rolled my eyes and dialed his number.

"Hello? Liz?" he answered groggily.

"Uh, hi. I guess I'm up for that call now," I stammered.

*What a stupid thing to say. I should have led with something along the lines of,* What the fuck, Jason? You're a married, dirty, rotten scoundrel, and I can't believe I let you smack my ass until I had the best damn orgasm of my life! You big asshole!

"Liz. Hey, sorry. I fell asleep a bit early. I guess it's the meds."

"Uh-huh."

Awkward silence.

If he was waiting on me to ask him about his arm, I wasn't. He could shove his burned and crispy arm up his ass for all I cared.

"I know what you saw in my file. It says I'm still married, doesn't it?"

"Yes." *Cold, quick, to the point. Gotta keep my head on straight. Even though I'm fuzzy as fuck.*

"Well, are you?" My tone was bitchy like I had just cracked a whip across his butt. His damn fine butt.

"That's the thing. I don't really know."

"What the hell does that mean? How don't you know if you're married? Was it some Las Vegas fling or something? Run off into the sunset, not knowing each other's last names, and parting ways, never to see each other again? Is your marriage not legal? Is she from another country? Are you? How the hell can you say you don't know?"

Enter drunk Liz—or as Team Jizz liked to call her, Ayesha. We weren't really sure why we had come up with that name, except for the fact that Ayesha sounded like a woman who would take no shit—ever, even if she was wrong—especially if she was wrong.

And for the safety of everyone around, please, dear Lord baby Jesus and all, please never tell Ayesha that she was wrong.

"No, I'm definitely from here. And … so was she. Where are you anyway? Are you out? I can come explain things in person. I actually prefer it that way."

"I'm at LA Jackson with Jess. You can come. We'll be here."

I noticed his use of past tense when he talked about his wife.

*She's dead. He's a widower. I'm a bitch.* I felt terrible.

"I know where that is. That's nearby where I work. Give me about an hour. Can you hang in there that long? I promise, I'll make it worth your while. I'm really sorry, Liz. I should have explained everything sooner. I just saw you that first night and things got wild and you were … an escape from that situation"

"The situation you're going to tell me and Jess about as soon as you get here? Because I tell her everything, and she knows what happened today. So, you can be examined by both of us. Does that work for you?" I motioned toward the waiter for a water refill.

"Of course. I would love to see y'all again. I could use some laughs and to get my mind off this damn arm of mine."

"See you soon then."

"See you soon."

I hung up the phone.

"She's dead," I said, throwing my hands in the air.

"Nuh-uh!" Jess's mouth hung open. "Are you kidding me? His wife is gone, and here we are, talking so bad about him! Oh my. We're terrible! Straight to hell we go!"

"I know! I feel so bad now."

"Are you sure?"

"Well, no. But he said she *was* from here, not that she *is* from here. I don't know. He said he will be here in an hour and explain things."

"This is going to be awkward." Jess grimaced.

"Tell me about it." I tapped my foot under the table.

The time creeped by as I checked my phone every three minutes. *Anxiety.* It was a thing for me, my fatal flaw, my only weakness. Besides the two other weaknesses I liked to keep secret. Okay, fine. I'd admit, I had a plethora of weaknesses. Many more than tattooed men singing in my ear and hard liquor. I had to grit my teeth to admit I didn't like to apologize. Which was what I was going to have to do, hence the anxiety.

"How's that water treating ya? You good? Sober yet?" Jess asked as I guzzled my third glass.

"Getting there! You?"

The nurse in me examined her for signs of drunkenness. With Jess, it was always slurred speech, of course, and narrowed eyes. She always looked as if she'd forgotten to wear her glasses and had to squint to see everything. Typical, normal drunk behavior, except she didn't wear glasses. She was just drunk.

"Same. I have a feeling we'll sober up real quick once Mr. Jones arrives." She nodded, still squinting.

"Speak of the devil." I straightened up and kicked her under the table. My eyes pointed in the direction over her shoulders.

Jess got the point and immediately tried to look busy with a napkin, failing miserably at her fake source of distraction.

*What the hell is she doing? Making a napkin swan? A hat? Waving a white flag of surrender? Damn, her lightweight ass is going to need a lot more time—and water.*

"Hello, ladies." Jason bowed. "May I have a seat?"

He glanced at Jess's napkin that she had thrown in the air in a fit of panic and that had come down, landing across her chest as a makeshift, dirty, lopsided bib. I blinked in a moment of shame for my dear drunky friend and decided to push more water on her.

"Yeah, of course. Come sit. How's your arm?" I asked, truly concerned.

However, I was more concerned, at the moment, with the reason he had come here. My feet had been jingle-jangling under the table, and if he didn't tell me what was up soon enough, I was going to have a full-blown panic attack at my favorite bar, and then I could never show my face here again.

*And I like these cocktails and this charcuterie, damn it.*

"It's been better, but I'll survive. I've got the day off tomorrow, so at least I have a little time to rest it," he said, looking over at Jess.

She sat quietly. Her arms crossed over her chest as she leaned back and inspected him with her drunken, narrow eyes. I knew I was going to have to relay this whole story back to her tomorrow because she wouldn't remember a thing. I stopped the waiter for more water and an order of fries for Jess. I knew what she needed. I had done this more times than I'd like to admit and more times than she'd like to admit too.

*Team Jizz!*

"Anyway, I'm not here because of my arm. You both know why I'm here. I feel like I'm under interrogation with you two, but here goes. I don't know if I'm married anymore. I think I am, but she's been gone for four years. Kate, my wife, left me four years ago. I came home one day, and she was just gone. No note, no phone call, no nothing. She never answered my texts or calls. I'm assuming she changed her number. No withdrawals out of our account. Just nothing. She ghosted me. We'd been married for only a little over a year. No arguments or anything that would have led up to her just up and walking out like that."

"Oh my gosh. That's horrible! Do you think she's okay? I mean, you're sure she left and—" I said, immediately ten times more interested. Did I ever mention that I was a fan of mysteries?

"No foul play? No. Nothing like that. I alerted authorities. They did their thing. It took months, but they declared that they were ninety-nine percent sure she'd just left. Said it happens. I still put the word out for missing persons. I searched for years. Honestly, I never gave up hope, and I had been searching until … well, right around the time I met you."

"Really? So, you've been looking for her for four years?" Jess asked between her mouthfuls of fries.

Finally, I could see her eyes straightening out.

"Pretty much. She was my wife. I loved her. I've held hope out for a long time, but at what point can I move on with my life, ya know? I would love some closure on the situation. Answers, anything. But I've got nothing." He paused, rubbing his palms down his jeans. "I couldn't wait around any longer, and besides, even if she walked back into my life tonight, I wouldn't take her. Not after she ghosted me like she did. So, here I am. Unsure of if I am married or not. But for my own sanity, I've moved on."

"Do you still look for her? Have you completely given up?" I said, my elbows not politely on the table as I leaned into this fascinating and heartbreaking story.

"I've completely given up. I can't put myself through it anymore. I don't think she would want me to do that anyway. If I'm being honest with myself, I can see her walking out. She had a gypsy soul; we often joked about it even. I think the wife life just didn't suit her. I just wish she'd talked to me about it, and we'd actually gotten divorced instead of me wasting years searching and wondering. I hope she's okay. I really do. I think she is. I like to think that she's on some tropical island with some hot dude named Pedro." He shrugged.

The silence that fell on our table wasn't awkward, but it was more of a deep sadness. He must have felt it, too, as I noticed his shoulders slumped even lower.

"I now consider it a blessing in disguise," he continued. "That heartbreak translated into my songs and got me to where I am today. We all grow from pain, and I'm very happy at this point in my life. I've done a lot of growing these last few years."

"I'm so glad you're at a good place now, and I'm really sorry for judging you without giving you a minute to explain yourself, Jason," I apologized— sincerely this time and without gritted teeth. I'd put Ayesha to bed.

I could see how uncomfortable he still was. I felt his feet, too, shake under the table. His knee bobbed up and down, fidgeting.

"That's all right. I totally understand, and hey, I'm here now, explaining things, so you did give me that opportunity. And thank you for it. I don't like talking about it, but I guess if I'm jumping back into the dating pool, I have to."

Jess looked from me to Jason and back again.

*What is she plotting?*

"So, you consider yourself available now and on the market? Did you sign divorce papers?" Jess smiled toward me but talked at him.

"I've not had a chance to get the papers in order yet, but I'm working on that. As far as dating, I've not been available long, but I've had one or two *dates.*" His face blushed.

I could even see it in the dim light. I knew exactly what his dates were. Hell, I'd had a date with him then too.

*Best date ever. And now, I can possibly have another? And another? And another?*

"I'm sure you'll have all the ladies after you. I mean, I know you already do. Obviously, from what I saw the other night," I said.

"Maybe. But see, there's this super-hot one I want after me. She's a really dirty nurse. Super dirty. And also super awesome. Someone I could actually date and get to know. Think I should ask her out? Take my chances? Seeing as how I am available and not the asshole she might have thought I was?"

*Oh my panties!*

"She says yes. The naughty nurse says yes!" Jess blurted, nodding toward me.

I could feel the fire burning in my cheeks.

"Unless there is some other naughty nurse you're talking about that you met today, and if there is, let me tell you this; she ain't got nothing on Liz. Liz is the filthiest, dirtiest, nastiest of nasty nurses. She will give you nights you won't ever forget!"

"Thanks … *friend.*" I gave Jess the side-eye. "Jason, I apologize. I'm so sorry for what my *friend* thinks is being a good wingwoman."

I noticed his body relax as he sat back and laughed at Team Jizz. If he was going to hang, he would have to just accept us for who we were even if we didn't have a clue of exactly who or what we were.

"I think you're right, Jess. I think I'll do it. She *is* amazing, and she's already given me a night I won't forget."

"You know I'm right here. This dirty nurse can hear it all. I'm not invisible!" I started to feel teamed up on between the two of them.

"Liz, it's impossible for you to be invisible. You're my front-and-center-stage gal. So, how 'bout that date?" He leaned in and eye-fucked me with those big blues of his.

*I'm his front-and-center-stage gal?* I felt myself start to melt.

"I'll bring the riding crop," I said, not missing a beat.

# 4

**JASON**

I lay in bed the next morning, thinking of how my week had gone from shitty to … *exciting? Relieving? A new start?* I felt like a different man after I'd gotten my story out and into the open, but I still couldn't believe I'd actually told them about Kate. I had been for sure one of them—or both of them—would throw a drink in my face. Liz seemed like she could be feisty, and damn if I did like feisty. Someone I could explore kinks with? Sign me up. Kate hadn't been like that with me. She was always too distracted with whatever it was she was distracted with. She was never down to even begin exploring her wild side, and I knew she had a wild side. I'd seen glimpses of it before—just not with me.

She had been wild and free before—on our honeymoon, at a resort in Bali, and once when we were taking dance lessons for our upcoming wedding.

She was adventurous back then—with those two other men anyway. I could tell by the way her body moved, the way her eyes shimmered, and the way her lips parted that she had a secret, seductive side that I didn't know about. She hadn't had that with me. I guessed I just didn't do it for her. But to be fair, I hadn't had that with her either. We were *friends*, and I still loved her like my wife. But when we'd made love, it had been … good, not great. There were definitely no spankings in our fuck sessions. That was something I had always wanted to try. Along with a million other things I hadn't yet had the chance to do or the partner to explore with.

*Until now at least … I think.*

Liz would be more than willing to explore with me; I knew it. With her fun attitude, willing body, and that perfectly pouty mouth … damn, that beautiful mouth of hers—blushing pink lips on her face and between her thighs. I felt my cock harden just by the mere thought of her. I wondered what it'd feel like to slide into that slick mouth of hers. Her doll eyes looking up at me while I fucked her mouth … all smiles while I filled her up. My dick jumped in my pants.

*Three more days, and maybe she will,* I thought.

I didn't even know if I could wait that long. If she had been that wild on a first one-night stand, how wild would she be for me when I took her out on a proper date?

I crossed my fingers in hopes that she would be exactly what I needed—someone to help me get over Kate.

I closed my eyes and stroked my cock, thinking of just how much I needed Liz right now. I fantasized about the way my hands would tangle in her hair as her head bobbed up and down under the covers. Her hands would work the base of my dick while she twirled her velvet tongue over the tip. My pulse quickened, my hips thrust forward, and my ass cheeks clenched as I came hard, imagining a wet and sloppy blowie from my dirty little nurse. I was a bit shocked at how fast I had come. Too fast. That wouldn't work for date night.

*I'm going to have to work on that,* I thought as I hopped up with renewed energy and headed toward the shower.

Luckily, I had three days to crank one out. Maybe I would be able to last longer then.

I made my way to work in a much better mood than usual. Brad couldn't even fuck with me today. Definitely not today. Even my arm felt like it had magically been on a quick mend.

"So, how's our hazardous employee and his arm? Not gonna hear from your attorney, am I?" Brad said, acting as if he were teasing me, but obviously, knowing Brad, he wasn't.

"No, definitely not involving my attorney in this one. Just not worth it." I smiled at him.

He so wasn't worth it.

"Good! Back to work you go!"

*Only for a little longer,* I sang in my head—yet another lyric. I scribbled it down on a napkin and tucked it into my back pocket.

These pieces of hastily written music were scattered everywhere around my house. I should just pick up a small notepad and sit my ass down and copy them in there, but I never seemed to have the time for that. I was too busy being a coffee master by day and a lyrical badass by night. I barely had time to sit, let alone organize. I was really bad at that anyway. I wondered if Liz was an organized person or if she was a spaz like me. My mind drifted to her again and back to reality as soon as I started with the steam.

I could see Brad as he watched me from his sad corner throughout the day. My wide grin and pep in my step sent him into an even worse mood. I didn't take it personally. Brad hated everyone. I enjoyed being happy around him, not because I thought it would rub off on him—I knew it wouldn't—but because the happier everyone else was, the unhappier he was. And, well, he was a shithead.

*So, suck it, Brad,* I thought as I smiled my way through the morning rush. I sang under my breath and danced around the counter.

"Well, someone is certainly feeling better!" Liz laughed and raised her eyebrows at my shameful antics.

"Liz." I grinned as I straightened myself up like I hadn't just embarrassed myself with my old-school Michael Jackson dance moves.

*I wonder if she knows it's her that's making me smile.*

"I came in to check on your arm—and your coffee skills." She stood tall in her scrubs that fit her banging body like a glove.

"Arm is good." I shrugged as I held my arm up for her to inspect. "But coffee is better. What can I get you?" I said, aware of Brad's eyes on the exchange between Liz and me.

I glanced at his seething face in the corner as he eavesdropped on our conversation.

"I have basic-bitch tendencies, so I would say a white chocolate mocha, but … I feel like trying something new. Branching out from the vanilla and all. I want something a little …spicier," she said as she traced her finger over her collarbone and gently tugged her neckline.

*And there it goes. My dick is hard yet again. This woman is driving me wild.*

"Oh, you're anything but basic. But, yeah, let's move you out of the ordinary vanilla lattes and into something spicier. Do you like tea?"

"I do. Whatcha plannin'?"

"Have you had chai tea?" I grabbed a container off of the shelf and showed her my absolute favorite drink. Besides vodka. And beer. And gin. And whiskey.

"I have! I love chai tea."

"Okay. Well, have you had … *dirty* chai tea?" I winked.

My cock pulsed in rhythm with my heartbeat. *Boom, boom, pow*—the *pow* being the little jump they both gave, trying to squirm their way over to Liz … like a fucking moth to a flame. Her redheaded flame.

"No, but this sounds interesting. Dirty, you say? I think I'll try it." She bit her lip, watching my every move.

I even saw her eyes drift down to my pecker in my pants—not once, but twice. Yeah, you could say I was on top of the world today.

I wondered just how wet she was getting, standing there, knowing my dick was hard for her. I longed to run my hand along her panties to see how slippery she was for me.

*Boom, boom, pow!*

"Don't you want to know what's in it before you order, miss?" Brad's limp-dick-inducing voice called from his dark corner.

"No, thanks! I trust Jason knows exactly what I like," she answered as she turned toward him, her head held high, her posture stiff.

She must have sensed his narcissism. He would never make it with the women. Not with his shitty attitude that hit you like a brick as soon as you were within earshot of him. He took one look at her *try me* expression and retreated back into his corner.

"Now, where were we?" she said as she watched me make her drink.

I knew she was probably still checking out my thick bulge under my apron. I didn't care. I wanted her to.

"I was telling you about a dirty chai. It's the espresso that makes it dirty."

"Dirty and buzzed? Count me in. Better put two shots of espresso in there for good measure. Twelve-hour shift today." She sighed.

She couldn't fool me though. I knew she loved her job. I could see it in the way she talked about it and in the way she'd worked when I was there as a patient. Besides, I suspected a twelve-hour shift was nothing for Liz. She could go all day and all night. She wasn't one to stop.

"Let me know how you like it." I handed over her drink while we grinned across the counter at each other like two goofy teenagers.

She took a slow sip and licked her lips—even slower. My cock was still pulsing and now dripping in anticipation of sliding between those silken lips of hers.

*I'm going to have to change my drawers if she keeps this up!*

"Mmm-mmm-mmm! I knew you would satisfy me. It's delicious."

"You're delicious," I whispered low enough so that the beast in the corner wouldn't throw a tantrum.

Liz giggled and pulled out her wallet. "Ring me up, and I'll get out of your way."

"It's on me. I'm just glad you like it. Hope you become a regular customer. Maybe branch out a bit and start exploring more options? I've got a full menu for you to try."

"Considering this place is on my way to work, I might. I really do need to explore more. So much more." She nodded, took a sip of her drink, and raised it up in a salute. "Three days. See you soon, Jason! Thank you for the morning buzz!"

"Anytime, Liz. See you soon!" My mouth watered as she did her signature sashay out the door.

I was in a trance until Brad coughed loudly and brought my thoughts back to the curious customer in front of me.

It seemed like I had just woken up and jerked off as I thought of Liz, and I was already back at home, doing it again. I couldn't help myself. Hopefully, all this fiddling my diddle would prove useful in lasting longer on date night. I couldn't even think straight with all the dirty thoughts in my head. I *had* to take care of my needs so that I could relax. I settled in for a quick wank before dinner and let myself think back to Liz in her scrubs and playing naughty nurse.

*Boom, boom, pow! Pow-pow-pow!*

I quickly finished up, much more quickly than I would have liked. I was a work in progress. I had things to do, and first on the list was the biggest task ever—cleaning. If I ever brought Liz back home to my place, I was going to have to get it sparkling. It wasn't terrible, but there was some dog hair and dust bunnies and spills on the wood flooring that had been there for who knew how long. It was a bachelor's pad after all. It could use some sprucing up for sure, especially after Deuce had been around.

I opened the windows for some fresh air and cracked a beer to get myself started. Deuce lay on his lazy butt and followed me around with his eyes. No doubt he was wondering just what the fuck was going on. I'd never been on a cleaning frenzy before.

Not even Kate had sparked this side of me.

*Kate* … I thought for the first time since last night. I had gone almost all day without even a thought of her. That was a first. I wasn't quite sure how I felt about that.

I opened my second beer and took a deep breath.

I went from room to room and searched for Kate's things as I carried a large trash bag with me. Her perfumes and makeup went into the trash. Her pillow went into the trash. Her toiletries and hippie soaps she'd loved also went into the trash. I spent two hours alone in the closet, working up a good buzz that I felt I needed in order to get rid of *her* and her things.

*Closing this chapter of my life. But am I really? Can this be it? Can Liz be the person I need to move on? And is that all she is? Just a catalyst in this? Or can she be something more? Do I want something more?*

Deuce sat up, still watching me from his bed.

"She's gone, boy. No use in keeping this stuff around anymore. It's just me and you." I sighed.

Kate hadn't much liked Deuce anyway. No matter how hard he'd tried to be her BFF, she wasn't having it. She'd been more of a cat person. That should have stopped me from marrying her right there.

"Come on," I said as I motioned him toward the door.

I carried five bags of Kate out to the trash and out of my life. I stopped in the hall to rid my home of one last thing—our framed wedding photo. It had been my favorite one out of the bunch. She'd had it mounted and put in a fancy frame soon after we were married. I still wasn't sure if she had done that because she felt like it was the wifely thing to do or because she really was proud of it. No matter, I'd still walked by it several times a day, every day, from then until now.

I pried it off the wall, surprised at how hard it was to take it down—in all the ways. I stood and looked at it for longer than I'd ever admit. My back leaned against the wall as I slid down into a slump. I sat and stared at the once-happy couple some more. I tried to let it go, but I couldn't do it. It wasn't trash. It was a piece of myself that had shaped me into who I was today. I just couldn't get rid of it. Not yet. I placed it on the top shelf of the closet.

Maybe, one day, I could look at it, but for now, I needed to move on even if that meant I wasn't able to fully let go—yet.

I spent the rest of the night in silence. The picture haunted me from the top of my closet. My thoughts, unfortunately, went back to Kate.

I had thought I was ready only moments ago. At least until the damn picture had set me off.

I rubbed my eyes and shook my head, trying to get ahold of myself.

I didn't want to be alone. I wanted Liz.

*But would she want me when I was clearly still confused about my marriage—or lack thereof?*

I decided to go to bed and sleep it off. Tomorrow, I would clean some more. Maybe I could pick up a few things for the house. It needed something to make it less … empty.

# LIZ

Maybe it was all the caffeine I'd consumed or the extra-long streak of sunshiny days or the newfound energy I had for working out, or maybe, just maybe, it was him. Maybe he was the reason I was high on life right now. He had put the pep in my step and given me the motivation I needed to get off my ass. I couldn't look like a busted can of biscuits next to Mayor McMuscle. If I kept shoveling barbeque nachos in my mouth, he wouldn't be able to pick me up and pin me against the wall, and I so wanted to do that. It was still on the list.

Of course I had a fantasy list. Didn't everyone? And if they didn't, did that make me a big whore? And if so, did I care? No, and no. I was getting too old to give any fucks about what people thought of me. My energy and focus had now been funneled into giving Jason all my fucks. Fucks against the wall, fucks outside, fucks in the car, fucks in the shower, fucks on the phone. All the fucks … but wasn't he still legally married? That would certainly put a damper on things.

I still wondered about her—Kate. *Kate the great* was probably what he'd whispered to her in bed after they made love. And then she'd just jumped up and walked out on him? There had to be more to the story, and like I'd said, I loved a good mystery.

Jess knew this about me, too, and before I could even bring it up, she had already told me, "Don't you dare go meddling! Just leave it. *Que sera, sera*, Liz."

But she also knew that I rarely listened to anyone's advice. I was stubborn like a bull.

*Kate Jones*, I typed in my phone's search bar as I waited on Jess for our lunch date. My boredom and curiosity had gotten the best of me. *I really shouldn't be left to my own devices.* I scrolled through page after page of non-relevant Kates. *Ugh, such a common name.*

Trying my luck again, I typed *Kate Jones, Nashville.* I still had nothing.

*Kate Jones, Jason Jones, Nashville,* I hurriedly typed before Jess came by to bust me. *Bingo!*

The first page that popped up sent chills down my spine. It was one of those mushy wedding pages. I guessed they never took it down. I quickly clicked on it before I even had a chance to really think about what I was doing.

*Who am I kidding? I know exactly what I'm doing. Pulling a Liz and making trouble for myself.*

A picture of Kate and Jason graced the front page of their adorable—*gag*—website. They looked into each other's eyes and laughed as she held her hand up to show off her engagement ring. She was beautiful with long, dark hair and even darker eyes. She had sun-kissed skin and a tight, taut figure. I bet she had been his workout partner. They probably used to do those cute Instagram-worthy workout-partner poses together, high-fiving each other with each sit-up as she wrapped her legs around him.

I stared at her picture. She reminded me of someone, but I couldn't remember who. She looked like someone I had seen before.

*Maybe college? High school?*

I closed my laptop and sighed. This was one mystery that would just have to wait. I felt bad for Jason, but I wondered if there was more to the story.

*How can anyone walk out on such a gorgeous man as him? Is he some crazy asshole behind closed doors? Does he have big issues, like a ton of debt? Or a nose-picking problem? Is his mother overbearing? Is there a secret baby?*

I had so many questions, yet I wasn't going to be the one to ask him.

*Maybe I should just take off my detective hat and see that whatever happens, happens this time?*

*Nah.*

"I know that look. What are you plotting?" Jess plopped down in front of me and grabbed a menu. "And where are the barbeque nachos?"

"I'm on a diet," I replied. "Besides, who needs barbeque nachos when you can have a Jessica Rabbit waistline?"

"First of all, you do know that Jessica Rabbit isn't real, right? She's a fucking cartoon! Second of all, you're at a barbeque place. What are you going to eat? A cracker?" She motioned to the packets of crackers on the table that had been left sad and untouched—like me.

"Nope. That would be carbs. Duh!"

"Oh my gosh. You don't need to diet!" She took a long drink of the sweet tea I had so graciously ordered for her.

Damn, I was such a good friend.

"You do know that Jason Jones has abs I can wash my laundry on, right?"

"You got me there." She shrugged. "He does have that hot fireman body. So, is that why you have resting bitch face? Because you're hangry as fuck and not eating?"

"Maybe." I grinned.

She was going to kill me.

"Uh-oh. What did you do?"

"Well … I've been such a good girl for so long. I didn't look her up once since he told us, but—"

Jess put her elbows on the table and her head in her hands. "You're impossible. But, kudos, I guess, for waiting, what, two days maybe?"

"Three. And I need your help. She looks familiar. I think I might have gone to school with her, but I can't tell him I think she looks familiar because then he will know I've been snooping and think I'm a crazy stalker!" I threw my hands in the air.

*Maybe I am getting a big hangry,* I thought as I felt the frustration bubble up inside me.

"Do you know what you'd like to order?" A very young waiter interrupted my meltdown. His eyes were wide with …

*Terror? Do I really look that crazy when I need to eat now?*

"I'll take the turkey leg, please. No sides. Just the leg. Thanks." I smiled as I tried to put him at ease. Instead, I felt like I was just baring my teeth.

"Barbeque nachos for me!" Jess handed him the menus, and he quickly scurried off. "Show me," Jess said as she nodded toward my phone. "I know you have her picture. Let me see it."

I pulled out my phone and took a deep breath as I handed it over to Jess. If I knew who Kate was, I was sure Jess would know who she was too.

"Wow, she's gorgeous. And, yeah, I'm guessing she definitely didn't eat barbeque nachos. Good call on the turkey leg."

"Damn it, Jess. Way to make me feel second rate."

"Kidding, kidding. Kind of." She laughed while she studied Kate's picture. "They look so … happy. I wonder what really happened. Think he's telling the truth about her leaving? What if he … oh gosh!"

"See? It's smart of me to look into all this for my safety. He could be a serial killer!"

"Safety first, I suppose. But I don't think he's a serial killer. I definitely think there has to be more to the story though. How can anyone just up and walk out? Just ghost someone like that?"

"My thoughts exactly. But does she look familiar to you?"

"Nope. Not at all. She's really beautiful. I would probably remember her if I knew her."

Jess sat back in her chair and folded her arms. "I think you should just leave it for now though. Be safe, but leave Kate out of it for a while. Let's see what happens over date night and maybe he will open up a bit more about it. I know that's going to be hard for you to leave alone, but just do it. Don't set yourself up for getting hurt, but be safe."

"I'll have to sit on my hands to keep from diving into this mystery, but fine! I don't want to get hurt. I like Jason. A lot. I don't want to think about him in love still … if that's the case."

"He did seem a bit … not over her. The way he talked about her, it was almost like he had some hope left, even when he said he didn't," Jess said out loud what I had been thinking as she shrugged.

"You picked up on that too? Damn. I thought it was just me. Crap."

"Poor Jason. His wife just ran out on him with no explanation, and here we are, talking about him being a serial killer. The man can't catch a break. Not to mention, his burned arm."

The waiter came back around and hurriedly set my turkey leg down in front of me before he ran off again.

"I'll give him the benefit of the doubt on date night. But only until date night. If he doesn't bring it up, I'm back to Detective Liz," I said as I pointed at Jess with my turkey leg.

With my mouth covered in barbeque sauce and meat nestled in between my teeth, I gave Jess a goofy grin to hopefully lighten the darkening mood.

She laughed as the waiter made his way to our table, and he quickly turned back around when he saw my meaty grin. Jess took a nacho and smeared it on her lips, drawing a smile two times bigger than her own.

"Think he will finally refill my drink now?" She laughed.

"Oh my! Maybe. Let's get him back over here," I said as I waved my turkey leg in the air to call for his attention.

It was obvious he'd been actively trying to avoid us, the two crazies in the corner, until another waiter shoved him in our direction.

"Excuse me, sir, but I'd like some more of that delicious sweet tea."

Jess smiled at the waiter. Her cheesy grin was literally cheesy. The kid looked as if he was about to cry.

"Me too, if you don't mind!" I chimed in, keeping a straight face as barbeque sauce dripped down my chin. "And wet wipes. Lots of wet wipes. My hands are so messy! How's my face, Jess? Anything on it?" I jutted out my chin for her to see.

The waiter stood there as he wrung his hands. His eyes glanced at me, down to the floor, up to Jess, and back down to the floor. I thought we were about to send this fellow into cardiac arrest. Lucky for him, I was a nurse.

"You look fabulous, as always, darling! I think I need some wet wipes for my hands, too, please, if you don't mind," she said as she looked up at him. The cheese had started to form a crust on her face.

He nodded, slowly backed away, and ran off toward the back.

Jess and I took a look at one another and almost fell out of the booth, laughing. The waiter jogged back by in a flash and threw the wet wipes on our table as we still were in hysterics.

"We are so terrible. Teasing that poor teenage boy like that!" I said as I cleaned the grease and sauce off of my face.

"Maybe you should have your date here. Pull that little stunt on him," Jess said in between mouthfuls of nachos.

"And send him running for the hills? No, thanks. Mr. Jones needs to see me at my best. That reminds me. Will you help me pick out a dress? I'll send over some photos later today, and you tell me which sends the signal that I'm interested, I need to be fucked, but I'm worried you're psycho, and I need to get to know you … all at the same time."

"Good luck with that! Sure, I'll help though. Luke will give you his opinion too. He is actually just as into this mystery as you are. Maybe you two can crack the case … *after* date night."

"Yes! After date night," I agreed.

I hoped date night would give me all the answers I needed. It would really suck if Mr. Jones was really Mr. Asshole, who had run his wife off. He was clearly into dominating, but I never got any bad vibes from him when he had his hands on my ass. And, damn, his hands on my ass had felt incredible. I'd take a spanking from Mr. Jones any day.

# 5

**JASON**

*Here goes nothing,* I told myself as I double-checked my reflection in the rearview mirror and smoothed back my hair.

This was my first official date as a single—kind of married and kind of not—man. My heart started to race as I grabbed the bouquet I'd picked up earlier. It'd only taken me about thirty minutes of pacing the florist's floor to pick something out.

*"What kind of message are you trying to send to her, sir? Maybe I can help put something together for you," the woman working the counter offered.*

*"It's a first date, so ... I guess something simple? I don't need to try to impress her. Just something sweet. But not overly romantic like red roses."*

*I tapped my chin, thinking. I tended to do that a lot—the chin-tap thing, not the thinking. I should probably do that more often.*

*"Ah, okay. So, first date … let's see." The woman smiled sweetly as she ran around the shop, grabbing this and that.*

*I wondered if she could throw a flower in there that said,* Let's fuck like animals again, *but I didn't want to be shooed out of here. I had to get the flowers. At least, I thought men still brought flowers to first dates, and if they didn't, they damn well should. Maybe it was the old soul in me or the dreamy musician, but I firmly believed in being a gentleman and having proper manners, no matter how old school that way of thinking was these days. The florist rang me up with a big, beautiful all-yellow bundle of flowers. If this couldn't make Liz smile, I didn't know what would.*

I cruised down Liz's street, searching out her address until I pulled up in front of a well-manicured lawn. *This has to be it.* I hopped out of my car and looked at her text again, comparing it with the address on the door in front of me before I worked up the nerve to ring the doorbell. My hands slightly trembled as I clutched the bouquet of sunshine.

Even I wished I'd gotten these flowers—if I were into that sort of thing and all. *Cough, cough, drink beer and roar manly stuff, cough, cough.*

But, really, men did appreciate beauty, too, and boy did I ever realize that was the truth when Liz opened the door. Her lustrous auburn locks flowed down her bare shoulders. Her legs were long, seemingly going on forever under that short, tight skirt. She smiled at me with her dazzling pearly whites, and my whole body suddenly felt on alert. The flowers didn't even do her justice. Nothing could do her justice. I'd never seen a woman so beautiful in my life. Especially not one who could send an electric spark down my body and out through my toes just by her smile alone.

"Hey! Come in, come in!" She ushered me inside.

I was instantly intoxicated as I caught a whiff of whatever it was she was wearing. *Peaches? Cream? Cinnamon? Did she make a peach cobbler, or is that her perfume? Damn, Liz is perfection. I really hope there's peach cobbler.*

"Here, these are for you," I said as I handed her the flowers and gave her a quick peck on the cheek.

"Wow! What a gentleman! I would have never guessed someone as kinky as you could be so sweet and thoughtful too! Thank you! These are gorgeous!"

"You don't think a man can be both?" I arched my eyebrows at her, hoping for a bit of playful banter.

"Not in my experience!" She rolled her eyes. "Have a seat. I'll put these in a vase, and we can be on our way. Won't take but a second."

I sat on her white couch and gazed around the room at the many pictures that were perched on bookshelves. I admired the glittery art that hung on her walls and nosily read the titles of the books that lay on her table. I could learn so much about her just by sitting here for thirty seconds. She liked contemporary art, and she read a variety of books, including classics, romance, and history. She had some little ones in her life.

*Nieces? Oh gosh, I hope so. Is she a mom?*

I started to freak out a bit as I stood up to take a closer look at the picture on her bookshelf. Two little girls sat on a swing, smiling. They both looked familiar.

"It's me and Jess," she said, catching me off guard.

*Phew. No kids,* I thought. It wasn't that I didn't want kids. I just was in no way, shape, or form prepared for them—yet.

"I thought those two looked familiar. Y'all must have been even more trouble back then. How long have you known each other?"

"Forever. We were born a day apart in the same maternity ward. That's how our moms met and became BFFs and insisted we did too. Luckily, we liked each other. So, it all worked out." She picked up her handbag and headed toward the door. "Ready? I'm starving!"

"Ready as ever! I made us reservations away from the honky-tonks and somewhere a little classier. You okay with that?" I said as I helped her up and into my truck.

Thankfully, I'd cleaned it meticulously beforehand; otherwise, it would have smelled like old Nashville hot chicken and stale fries. Which could also be found tucked here or there under a seat or two ... along with dog hair.

"Hey! Just because I'm Team Jizz doesn't mean I can't be classy!"

"That's not what I meant at all," I stammered.

We hadn't even made it to the date, and I was already putting my foot in my mouth.

"I'm just messin' with you, Jason! I can be classy as fuck. Watch me," she teased. Her posture straightened up as she crossed her legs, pursed her lips, and put her nose in the air.

"I said classy, not snobby! But that actually looks good on you too. Anything would look good on you.

You could be a grade-A bitch and still be drop-dead gorgeous."

It was true. I could barely even concentrate on driving with her beside me. Anything would look good on her—or off of her.

"Grade-A bitch, huh? You've seen that side of me. Still feel bad about that, by the way," she muttered. Her lips turned down into a sad, little pout—still gorgeous.

"Hey, hey, hey! No, we aren't going down that road again. Fresh start. Deal?"

I reached over and grabbed her hand. I felt a spark run through me as soon as my skin touched hers—an energy so intense that the hairs on the back of my neck stood up. I'd not felt that in … the history of ever, and by the expression in her eyes, I didn't think she had either.

"Deal," she replied breathlessly.

# LIZ

I didn't know what it was about Jason that set my lady bits on fire, but he did. Scratch that. I totally knew what it was about Jason. It was his biceps, his sly grin, his tousled hair, and that sexy Southern drawl he had when he crooned his sweet songs. Also, those abs … and that cock.

*Damn, that cock. Am I going to get lucky tonight?*

I hoped so. I had taken the time to make myself ready at least, and by ready, I meant, I had performed gymnast tricks in my tiny shower to make sure I shaved every last piece of stubble growing on my biscuit.

I was smooth and silky and ready for anything he could throw at me. Speaking of throwing, I still really needed to be thrown up against the wall with my legs wrapped around him as he drove himself deep inside of me.

*Is that ever going to happen?* I mused on how I could drop the hint as we pulled up to the restaurant and made our way inside.

It was definitely a classy restaurant—like valet and nose-job classy, or steak and silicone classy. It was somewhere along the lines of *if I eat here, I'm going to need a house in the Hamptons and a dog I can stuff in my purse* classy.

Do people still do that even? I looked around the grand entrance and tried to find a pocket-sized pooch stuffed in a Louis Vuitton. No luck.

"I think this might be more than classy, Jason. I'm glad I dressed up! You gotta warn a girl next time! What if I had come here in some skinny jeans and a crop top?"

I smoothed my dress as he pulled my chair out for me.

"I somehow don't believe you'd go on a date in skinny jeans and a crop top. You are, or you seem, quite a bit more extra than that." He laughed.

"Oh my gosh! I'm so not extra!" Lies. I totally was.

I just didn't want him to know that, except I guessed he somehow already did. Maybe it was the stilettos that had given me away … or the blinging earrings that I'd decided to wear at the last minute. So what? I liked to appear nice, and maybe, just maybe, I also liked things that tended to shine and sparkle.

*Is that really a bad thing? For anyone or anything other than my bank account?* No, I didn't think it was.

I couldn't help that I leaned toward the finer things in life. I mean, I did wear scrubs all day, every day. That shit got old fast. Sometimes, it was nice to feel a little *extra*.

"Sure, sure. You're not extra at all." He winked. "I'm just sayin', if you own a pair of cowboy boots, they are pink and *might* have some glitter on them."

*Crap. Did he raid my closet? They aren't even pink though … just platinum.*

I folded my arms over my chest as I tried to hide my smile. I was going to stand firm. He would just have to accept this down-to-earth view of myself I had even if it was completely bogus.

"All right. Come on, Plain Jane. Let's get a drink. Will that be a beer or a fancy-schmancy craft cocktail?"

"Cocktail." I smirked.

"Ha!"

"What do you expect? You want me to guzzle a cold one at a place like this?"

"You're exactly what I expect. Beautiful, funny, smart, classy, and sassy. I like the attitude. It gets me … riled up."

He pulled at his collar and grinned. I needed to feel that grin with my lips.

"Thank you, Jason. You are every bit of dreamy too. I don't know if you've noticed, but you have all the women here drooling."

He looked around the room and smiled. He probably just set several women's panties aflame with that smile of his.

"They're probably drooling over their refreshing beers they ordered instead of a froufrou cocktail," he teased.

The waitress lazily made her way to our table to take our drink orders. Her eyes were only focused on Jason. If I didn't speak up, I doubted she would even know I was there.

"I'll take an old-fashioned, please. Rye whiskey, heavy on the bitters. Thanks." *Froufrou my ass,* I thought as I watched his eyebrows rise up into his hairline.

"I'll have the same," he said, nodding like he knew what he was doing.

I was going to have to show him I was definitely not a froufrou. I might be extra, as in I wanted to treat myself extra and expect to be treated extra, but I was *not* a stuck-up, silly-nilly froufrou. I could get down and dirty, and hopefully, by the end of the night, he'd see that side of me.

"So, Liz, how did you get into nursing? Tell me a bit about yourself."

He leaned in, seemingly interested … *in me?* I guessed this was how it was going to be then—a real date. I thought I must have expected more of a *Mr. Jones, come spank my booty* conversation, but he was taking things slow, and I respected that.

"It's not really an exciting story. My parents both were in the medical field, I fought hard against joining them and rebelled to art school, found out that wasn't my calling and that my calling really was in the medical field, so I switched to nursing school, and here I am." I shrugged.

He smiled at me.

*Does he ever stop smiling? That smile could light up this entire room, which would be great because it's dark as hell in here! Who can read these menus?*

"What about you? How did you get into singing? And coffee?"

"Well, the coffee is a shit job I took to learn the business. I have a shop I bought that I've been working on. No one knows about it, except you now."

"What do you mean, a shop? You have your own coffee shop?"

"Kind of. I work in there when I can, straightening the place up, getting it ready to open, ordering all the equipment, that type of thing."

"Wow, Jason. That's pretty awesome! Where is it at?"

"Very close to the hospital. Very, very close to the hospital. Within walking distance. So, maybe you just found your new morning coffee spot," he said. He took a sip of the old-fashioned that the waitress had just set before him. "Ooh-eee! Shit fire! That is—phew. That's good. And strong. Damn!"

I took a sip of mine and laughed. I could handle it, *and* I could handle him.

"I'm certainly planning on checking your coffee shop out. I could use a regular place. I tend to not commit to anything in particular. Well, except for my and Jess's favorite bar. Otherwise, I'm all over town. Never letting myself stop long enough to get to know a place." *Or person. Shit. What am I saying? He's going to think I'm talking about my commitment issues—and I am.*

*Damn, this drink is strong! But let's be real with myself here. It's not the drink. It's classic Liz getting scared and pushing away.*

I watched him watching me and my nonstop internal dialogue. His head was cocked to the side, much like a confused dog, as he tried to figure me out.

*Good luck with that.* I hadn't even figured myself out.

"Wanna see it?" he interrupted my musings.

"See what?"

"The coffee shop, silly. We can swing by after dinner. I've never taken anyone there. You can give me your opinion on some things, seeing that you have amazing style and all."

"Really? You think so? Aw, thanks! I'm flattered! I'd love to see your shop. And just so you know, I don't have pink cowboy boots in my closet."

"Oh, is that so? Well then, I guess I was wrong." He shrugged.

*Is it really that easy for him to admit when he is wrong? Keeper!*

"They're platinum." I laughed as I took another sip of my drink.

"Short skirt, fire-kissed hair, platinum boots. I'm going to write a song about you, ya know, if you keep on teasing me like that."

"Shit! I didn't even think about that! If I piss you off, I could end up in the next hit song all up and down Music Row. Crap." I was going to have to remind myself not to flip my bitch switch. I didn't want to be known as Loony Liz, the psychopath ex-girlfriend.

*Girlfriend? I'm getting ahead of myself here.*

"I make no promises as to where my music comes from. But I'll give you a hint. It's the heart. Comes from the heart. And sometimes, the soul. And also sometimes, after too many beers … or fancy craft cocktails."

He saluted me with his drink, and I instantly felt a tingle in my drawers.

*He is trouble. But that's okay because so am I.*

# JASON

It was bound to happen. Things had been going too good. It'd all been too good to be true—Liz, my stunning, smart, sexy, and funny date; the phenomenal food and drinks; the interesting conversations; the dark and sultry ambiance. Everything had been perfect—until it wasn't. My truck took a turn for the worse as it sat, stuck on the side of the road with a damn flat. Of course that would happen tonight of all nights! And if that wasn't bad enough, it started to rain.

"Well, fuck. I'm sorry, Liz! Hang tight. I'm going to get the spare on. Must have been those damn Nashville potholes! Guess I'll have to show you the café another time."

"You can't go out there in the pouring rain! Let's just wait it out. I'm sure I can think of a few things we could do to pass the time."

There was that grin of hers again. The one that meant trouble. I watched her as she innocently hiked up her skirt. Wow, she was really going in hard, just like I wanted to go in hard … in her.

*Maybe this night can be salvaged after all.*

At least we were stuck on a back road. There wasn't much traffic coming by at all.

"How can I resist you when you do something like that?" I said, reaching for her.

The jolt of our skin touching sent a warm flush throughout my body.

"I don't want you to resist me. I want you to ravage me. Preferably up against a wall, but I've never done this in a truck either, so—"

"So, you want to fuck in my truck in the middle of a rainstorm?"

"Maybe. Will this be in your lyrics about crazy Liz?"

"Not-so-crazy Liz. Liz, who I bet tastes …" I said as I leaned down to pull her panties to the side and get a lick. "Who tastes so fucking delicious."

I held her hips down as she squirmed against my lips. Her clit felt like velvet in my mouth. She was so fucking wet already. I buried my face in between her legs as I spread her apart with my hands. I grabbed her and pulled her into my mouth while I fucked her with my tongue.

Fuck, she tasted good. Like no dessert I'd ever had before. She was sweet like nectar on my lips. She was a flower—my flower.

"Fuck me, Jason. I need you," she whispered.

She pulled me up and began to unzip my pants. My cock slipped out of my pants as it throbbed with the need to feel her warmth wrapped around it. I stroked myself with my hand as she watched. Her hips bucked in the seat as she impatiently waited on me to fuck her senseless.

"There's a condom in there." I nodded toward the glove box before I quickly realized I'd just made a mistake. I was pretty sure time had stopped in that moment of realization of what was about to happen. I could see through the windshield that the raindrops were floating in midair, I heard a long and steady hum of thunder in the distance, and my face stayed frozen in anticipation. The only thing that time hadn't stopped was her hand from flipping the lever on that glove box, and then out popped … oh, about eight hundred and sixty-seven photos of my wife.

*Fuck.*

"*Oh,*" she said.

*Oh.* Yep. I was up shit creek without a paddle. And speaking of paddle, there wouldn't be any spankings tonight, except for me spanking myself— alone and in bed, as usual.

"Oh, that's, uh—that's, um … that's Kate. I should have cleaned that all out, but I totally forgot those photos were still in there. It was for the report, and I …" I stammered.

My cock was still out but was shriveling faster than old Uncle Ron's face after he got that lap-band thing we'd all warned him about. He'd damn near aged twenty-five years in a matter of days. Some people were just meant to be hefty. We *were* in the South. It was pretty much expected with all the bacon-fat double-fried chicken with a side of clogged arteries that seemed to be on just about every menu around here.

"She's beautiful," Liz said as she pulled her skirt back down and reached to pick up the pictures.

She thumbed through them as I sat and watched. My palms started to sweat as I tucked my sad sack of limp johnson back into my pants.

"She was."

"When you say *was*, how do you know she *isn't*? Do you think she's gone—as in dead? I'm sorry if that sounds harsh."

"No, I don't. I think she really did run away. I just have to tell myself that she *is* in the past—my past. So, for me, it is a *was* because she is a part of me that is no longer. Wherever she is," I said as I stared at a picture of the two of us.

It was a picture from the day I had proposed to her. We were happy and smiling. It was a warm spring day at the park. The geese behind us had been hissing and chasing us around. That was why she smiled and laughed. But I … I was smiling and laughing because of her. Even I could see it right then and there in that photo. My eyes were on hers, and her eyes were elsewhere.

"I'm so sorry, Jason," she said, still not looking up from the pictures she'd been studying.

"She looks familiar to me. Do you know where she went to college? Was she a nurse?"

"She never went to college. She had a restless soul. Taking odd jobs here and there and boring easily with the mundane day-to-day. She was quirky like that."

The silence that hung in the air was heavy, stifling. I cracked a window to get some fresh air. This wasn't going as planned.

"Hey, look. The rain's let up. Let me help you get the spare on. I'm pretty handy with tools," she said.

I thought about making a sexual innuendo to relieve some of the tension between us, but the moment quickly passed, and now, it would be awkward.

*Can't be fooling around while my wife is tucked neatly in my glove box. Kate, Kate, Kate. Will you ever be gone for good?*

My head swam with thoughts of Kate and thoughts of Liz as we stood in the middle of the misting rain.

"You don't have to help me, ya know! Get back in the truck. You'll get that pretty outfit of yours soaked out here."

"It's only rain! Besides, what do you think I am? A princess? I can change a tire too!" She stood with one hand on her hip and the other pointing that wrench at me like she was about to hold me hostage. I would gladly oblige.

"Oh, I bet you can. But that doesn't mean I want you to," I said as I cautiously took the wrench from her and got back to work.

"So, what do you want me to do? Just stand here, looking pretty for you?"

"Well, yeah. Actually, that would be perfect."

I felt the smile on my face stretching across my cheeks in probably the most idiotic grin. I couldn't help myself. Liz was hellfire stuffed inside a jeweled box. I was as much scared as I was turned on.

"Hmmph." She crossed her arms over her chest and narrowed her eyes while she watched me work.

*Am I imagining it? The hint of a smile behind those pursed lips? No way.*

Liz loved every bit of the banter too. She liked it rough—Mr. Jones–style. I knew this for a fact. She could play the tough superwoman role all she wanted, but in bed, she was mine.

*Fuck.* I felt myself getting hard. *I hope she's watching the road*, I thought as I glanced up to meet her eyes. *Nope, still watching me with that fixed gaze of hers.*

"There. All done," I said as I wiped my hands on a towel and stood up to meet her gaze.

Both of us had started to get soaking wet as the rain began to fall again in a slow drizzle.

She'd been standing there with her tough-girl attitude and stuck it out with me in the rain the entire time.

*And I thought, in the restaurant, she said she wasn't down to commit?*

I thought I was beginning to know her even if she didn't know herself.

I pulled her into me, the sticky rain like a wet, heavy blanket that weighed down on us both. I wanted to kiss her. I needed to kiss her.

This was the scene—the time to salvage the night. The dark, the rain, the mood, the sexual tension—all of it had been building up to this moment, and yet … I just stood there like a doofus. I was unable to move or take my eyes off of her. It was as if that fixed gaze of hers was some type of hypnotizing spell holding me there. I was suspended in a fit of lust and confusion.

"You're not over her, ya know," she whispered into my lips.

And just like that, I realized, maybe she was beginning to know me too …even if *I* didn't know myself.

*Crap.*

"I'm trying," I muttered as I closed my eyes and kissed her on the lips.

*I am so fucking trying.*

6

## LIZ

When I'd thought I would have answers to all of my questions on date night, I was right. Well, almost. I still had no idea what had happened to Kate, but now I knew Jason wasn't able to get over his wife.

I should have known it was too good to be true. That chemistry we had couldn't be real, not for now. Not until he had closure.

*Will he ever get closure?* Who knew? But I'd not allow myself to wait on him. It was the commitment issues.

Okay, maybe that sounded a bit harsh. But I'd waited around on men before, only to end up hurt. So, nope, not today, not this time, not ever. Coldhearted or not, Jason was just going to have to remain a friend with naughty panty-melting benefits. And, damn it, if my panties hadn't gotten melted last night either—yet again. It was almost as if the universe had tried to stop us. There'd been the flat tire, the rain … the wife.

*Can't a woman catch a break?*

I needed his electricity to course through my veins. I needed to not be able to feel my legs for a bit, to wobble around in a drunken post-sex stupor. I needed Jason—as just a friend … with benefits, of course.

> *Jess: So, are you even able to walk this mornin'?*
>
> *Me: Wow, you're up early! Call me. I am, unfortunately, able to walk.*
>
> *Jess: Boo, hiss.*

My phone rang immediately. Sometimes, I thought Jess lived vicariously through me, but when I saw her and her husband melted all over each other like two dollar-store popsicles, I knew I'd been kidding myself. She was a perv, just like me.

"So, what the fuck? No fuck? Where did he take you anyway? What did y'all end up doing?"

"Good morning to you too!"

"I mean, good morning, sunshine! Did you get pounded up against any walls last night or nah?"

"Let's see. We went to a super-fancy restaurant. I don't even know how to pronounce the name."

"Yeah, yeah. Go on."

"And then when we left, he was going to take me to a café he owns."

"A what? Hold up. Do what now? He has a café?"

"A little coffee shop. Not far from my work. Imagine that …"

"Uh, okay. So, you guys didn't get frisky in the coffee shop? That would've been … steamy. Ha-ha! Get it?"

"Yeah, I get it, ya big dork. And we never actually made it to the coffee shop. He got a flat tire!"

"Oh Lawd! How did y'all get home?"

"We both changed the tire. Well, I watched while he was all chivalrous and shit. It was actually kind of sweet. But anyway, that's not all. That's not really what made me dry up like the Sahara even if I was wetter than anything, standing out there in the middle of hell's downpour."

"So, what was it then? Spit it out."

"It was his wife. I reached to get a condom out of his glove box, and pictures of her fell out. She was staring straight at me while I had my skirt hiked up around my waist and my hooha out for all to see."

"Well, why didn't you just tell her, *My turn*, and pop her back in the glove box and be on your merry way?"

"Because of the look of sadness that I saw cross his face for a split second. He tried to play it cool after, but I had seen it. He still misses her. Still wonders."

"Jeez. Now what? I guess there's no going back from that. Gonna throw in the towel and move on or what? I think you might be setting yourself up to get hurt if you fall for a man who can't let go of his past like that."

"Exactly. I'll not be doing that to myself. I did tell him I wanted to still see his shop though. So, we're meeting tomorrow for lunch and heading over. I just have to keep myself in check. My heart and head. My loins—eh, not so much."

"But you know your loins are connected to your heart, and your head isn't anywhere around when that's happening. It's like your head goes on vacation, and your heart and loins have a party. Then, when shit goes down, your head comes back and is like, *What the fuck?*"

"How about you can be my head then?"

"Damn it, Liz."

"I'm just saying. If I decide to play a bit with him—not saying I will, but—"

"You will."

"Okay, I will. But I'm just saying, remind me not to get hurt if I start falling for him. You know, when he touched me, it was so electric. Like tiny tingles coursing through my blood."

I felt myself grow warm as I talked about Jason. My smile grew wider and wider, thinning my voice and making my lips quit working properly. He made all parts of me not work properly.

*Damn it.*

"You're already falling for him, *and* you'll get hurt. But sure, I'll be around and promise not to say I told you so. Instead, we can get drunk and eat ice cream when shit goes south. As usual."

"Speaking of going south, Jason's got a tongue that I swear vibrates. It. Is. Hot."

"Vibrating tongue, huh? That's a new one. Just be careful. Have fun but be careful."

"Always."

"No, not always. You never. It's never. So, this time has to be different."

"I'm pinkie-promising through the phone."

"Are you? You'd better have your pinkie out and wiggling it, damn it."

"Wiggle, wiggle. Cross my heart."

"Okay. Let me know how the lunch date goes."

I sighed as I put my phone down. She was right though. I had a history of heartache. It was as if I had a magnet inside my jangalang that pulled me toward unavailable men. Whether it was because they were cheating assholes, workaholics, baby daddies, or they traveled with a circus freak sideshow. Yeah, that was real. Yeah, that had happened. We didn't speak about it—ever.

I mentally put a cage around my heart and busied myself with my patients. I crossed my fingers in hopes of a fast-paced day to keep my mind off of Jason and his vibrating tongue. He was … all that and a bag of chips.

*Do people still use that line?*

Well, he was. And he wasn't just some plain, greasy potato chips. Jason was the Doritos of men— *the* chip.

*Damn, I'm hungry. This low-carb thing is for the birds,* I thought as I marched toward the vending machine.

## JASON

*Me: You like hot chicken?*

I texted Liz before I headed out to my place—Café à la Some Shit.

I hadn't even come up with a name for it yet. My head had been in other areas for so long that I hadn't had much time or energy to put into my little shop. But lately, with Liz, I felt … *motivated?* I often found myself going about my day, humming or singing, which hadn't been the norm for a very long time, especially for a singer like me. And when I caught myself humming recently, it was usually a song that had sprung from thoughts of her. All of the thoughts. Naughty thoughts, happy thoughts, dreamy thoughts, and thoughts about getting the *feels*—which, I had to admit, scared the shit out of me. But I knew it wasn't just me who'd felt the chemistry between us the other night.

The way her body had responded to my touch would forever be ingrained in my brain. That jolt that had gone through her and me—there was no denying that.

I checked my phone as it buzzed from my pocket. *A buzz.* That was what she was—a buzz—and I didn't want to lose the Liz buzz by sobering up to real life. I would happily continue being lust-drunk for the rest of my days.

> *Liz: Am I a Nashvillian or what? Of course I like hot chicken! Doesn't everyone like melting their innards from time to time? It's actually a pretty good cleanse.*

> *Me: Ha! It's not the most pleasant cleanse, but no worries, I'll get mild. Thought I could pick some up and you just meet me at the café. We can eat there. Sound okay?*

*Liz: Sounds perfect.*

*You're perfect*, I wanted to tell her.

She made me laugh, she made me throb, she made me ache.

*Is this a rebound?* It had all been happening so quick—at least for me.

I still had no idea how she felt. She was probably pretty damn shitty after the other night—our failed date night. But I really had been trying to get over Kate, and I thought Liz was helping with that, which was exactly what I wanted even if it came with *the feels* and even if I caught myself falling for her.

*Should I let her know that she is helping me get over Kate?*

I didn't know if that would be a terrible idea or not. I tended to put my foot in my mouth—often. The last thing I wanted her to think was that I was only using her. Sure, the original plan was for her to help me get over Kate, but that sounded bad, didn't it? I decided that I probably needed to keep that idea to myself. I didn't think Liz was the type of woman I would want to scorn. That was a road I would prefer not to go down.

*Those redheads … yikes.*

Don't ask. It was a fiasco I would love to forget—one that would be blazed in my memory to the end of my days.

Okay, fine. I could relive the whole terrible story.

This redhead I'd dated was crazy! In fact, she was the only woman I'd ever considered writing a song about. And not a good song either. Cindy … except I couldn't rhyme batshit crazy with Cindy, and then I just said fuck it. Let Cindy be Cindy. Which, like I'd said, was batshit crazy. And if I had written a song about her, I shuddered at the thought of what might have happened to me. Thankfully, she'd moved far, far away.

That relationship was pre-Kate. I could admit, I had been a bit of an asshole back then. Well, not really an asshole but just inexperienced in the whole dating field—and I also had wanted to play the whole dating field. I didn't know the rules, so—

Okay, that was a lie. I had known the rules, and I'd broken every single one of them because I was young, dumb, and ready to get laid every second of the day. Yep, that was me. Not anymore though. Well, the young part anyway. I'd be thirty-two this year, for fuck's sake.

Anyway, back to Cindy.

Cindy had caught me red-handed—*headed*—with Mindy. No, I couldn't make this shit up. Cindy had apparently known for a while about Mindy but wanted to make a big scene about it when the time was right. At least she had patience, I guessed.

She had to have had patience because she had been stealing my underwear for a long time. Wait! It got better. My *dirty* underwear. Anytime I'd invited her over, unbeknownst to me, she would grab a pair or two out of the hamper—or from the floor … because you know … I could be a lazy man. I never really wondered where my undies had been going. I just kept buying them and figured the dryer monster had eaten them like he had done with my socks sometimes.

Well, Cindy must have known Mindy would be coming over that day. I still didn't know how she had gotten inside my place. I was guessing she'd copied a key, but I wouldn't put it past Cindy to pick a lock.

So, Mindy and I got to fooling around, and we started to head toward my bedroom where my bed had a new quilt on it—made entirely out of my dirty underwear. But wait! There was more! Stitched on my undie quilt was, *Thanks for the shitty lay.* I kid you not! You could say it was funny at the time, but remember, we were talking *dirty* underwear here. There might have been some skid marks here and there, but only if you looked really, really closely.

So, you might be asking, *What kind of person takes time out of their day to go to the lengths to not only plan such revenge, but to also stitch a shit quilt?* Redheads. That was what kind of person.

I knew it took a lot of time to make a quilt. My grandma used to stitch them. Albeit not a shit quilt— to my knowledge anyway. Cindy must have worked day and night on that thing.

To be fair, she'd had other red flags too. I'd just ignored them because she was hot as fuck. Never again though. I'd learned my lesson on that one, and I'd also learned to invest in a bidet. I never heard from her after that until I saw a mutual friend congratulating her on her wedding on a Facebook post. That poor soul of a man ... who probably wasn't even a man anymore, but just a lump of ashes burned in the fury of Cindy's palm.

And that was my story on redheads. I doubted Liz would ever do something that crazy. Plus, she had the whole nurse/germ thing going for her. No way would she sift through dirty underwear just to make a point. Would she?

I paced the floors of the café, waiting on Liz to arrive. This would be the first time I showed anyone, other than local contractors, my place. I hoped she could see past the dust on the floors and the bare walls and picture what I envisioned for the café even though I wasn't even sure what I envisioned for the café— besides music and caffeine. I was clueless when it came to style.

Although jeans and a semi-fitted top were always my go-to, I sometimes ventured into new territory with my outfits. I wasn't sure I could call it *my* own personal style, as, most of the time, when I shopped at a department store for new clothes, I'd just copy the outfits on the mannequins.

*Suave suit? Hook me up.*

*Casual yet sophisticated country-club attire? Sure, I can do that.*

*Vacation style with the classic Hawaiian shirt? I'll wear it somewhere!*

So far, it'd worked well. I never had any complaints. Who needed a stylist when you could let the stores do it for you? Some might call it lazy, but I called it smart. And also, like I'd said, clueless.

"Knock, knock!" Liz stuck her head in the door.

"Come on in! Welcome to Chez Café à la Something or Other!"

"You don't have a name picked out yet?" she asked, stepping over a wood pile.

"Nope. Not yet."

"A lyrical genius such as yourself can't even come up with a catchy name?"

"Ha! Genius! You're funny. I don't write most of my own music, ya know. I only have a handful of songs that I've actually written. Anyway, come follow me and let me show you around before we eat." I motioned for her to follow me.

She stuck her hand out and touched the surfaces we passed, nodding in what I hoped was approval. I showed her the kitchen and coffee area, the sitting areas, the little stage where I wanted to book local artists, and my personal favorite, the patio.

"This is so awesome, Jason. I'm impressed! When will it be ready? I'm ready for it to open now! I want to sit over there in that corner and sip a latte while I listen to you sing on that stage."

"Who knows when it'll be open? But I'm hoping before the fall. I've still got a lot of work to do, as you can see. I've got a few more inspections to get through, furniture to order, more appliances to get, and I have no idea what kind of look I'm going for. I might need to hire a designer. I've also got hiring employees to think about. My buddy from the coffee shop will more than likely work here, but finding the right team is going to take a while too. And then I'd also like to do some type of community outreach event. Give back to the community and all. Maybe like a monthly charity gig or something. We'll see. I have a lot of ideas. I'm just not the best at time management. The café has been in this state for months."

"Wow. Yes, that's a lot. So, let's sit down and make a list while we eat. A to-do list. We can knock one thing off at a time."

"We?"

"I'll help. I mean, if that's okay with you. I believe in it—and you. You're going to rock this café. Plus, it needs to be awesome if I'll be here before work every morning. That is, unless you do something to piss me off, and then … well—"

"You'll burn the place down?"

"Jeez! No! What the fuck, Jason?"

"Redheads. I'm just saying."

"I was going to say, if you pissed me off, I might just bring a wrecking ball to it, but if it's fire you want, it's fire you'll get." She laughed.

"Don't I know it? You are fire! And speaking of fire, want some hot chicken?" I dangled the bag in front of her like it was some type of prize. It kind of was. I mean, who didn't like Nashville hot chicken?

"Oh my goodness! Did you get the piggy chips with it?"

"I knew we spoke the same language. Oink, oink. That means, fuck yes. Come sit down with me on …" I looked around the shop before I realized I was seriously unprepared for a lunch date here. "Shit! I'm sorry! I don't have any seats!"

"I can stand and just eat at the counter. No biggie."

"No, you won't. Come on, there's a bench outside. We can just be Neanderthals and use our laps. Next time, I'll bring the red Solo cups and a blanket. Picnic-style."

"I like that idea. Sounds like a plan to me!"

I held the door for her while I watched her sweet ass bounce to the patio. I loved to watch her walk. That pep in her step always got me riled up.

"Thanks for lunch, by the way. I appreciate it, and I appreciate you showing me your shop."

"It's my pleasure. And, Liz, I want to make up for the other night. Being caught in the rain and all. I was wondering, can I take you out again—soon? Something simpler. Maybe pizza and dancing?"

"First, it's hot chicken, and now, it's pizza. Are you trying to turn me into a butterball? You know the way to my heart has always been paved with grease … and maybe some vodka too."

"Is this a trick question? Because I do like that juicy ass of yours."

I took a bite of my sandwich and immediately felt my eyes begin to water. Surely, they hadn't messed up my order. I thought I'd ordered a medium-heat level. I glanced over at Liz, who had also just bitten into her sandwich. Her face turned an odd shade of purple.

"Holy shit! Did you order the extra-extra hot?" she said as she clutched her throat.

"No! I didn't. I think they messed my order up. Damn!" I choked back tears as I handed her a bottle of water from the take-out bag.

I guzzled my own water down as I made a mental note to stop and get some antacids before I headed home. I loved spicy food, but whatever seasoning was on this chicken had come straight from the pits of hell.

"You don't have to eat it! Here, have some of these piggy chips." I handed her a box stained with grease spots. The film it had left on my fingers gave me instant regret.

"I can handle it. Fire, right?" she said as she took another bite. Her face was still a scary shade of purple that I'd never seen before.

I continued eating and started to break out in a sweat. "Okay, firecracker, I see your resilient taste buds and match them with my own." I licked my fingers, wincing, and I was pretty sure my eyes had halfway popped out of my head at this point as well. Maybe I had the purple-face thing going on too.

We finished our meals in a state of competitive agony while she rattled off items she had thought needed to be done at the café. She fished out of her purse a pen and wrote our to-do list on the back of an old Target receipt.

I wondered just how much help she would be. It would be hard to get anything done around her.

I listened to her talk, but my gaze kept wandering to her lips—those beautiful, spicy lips.

"And then I think you should do some industrial-style barstools and then maybe—are you even listening to me?"

*Busted.*

"I am! I just so love the way you get excited and how the little corners of your mouth get wider and wider and wider. It makes me excited, and then I lose my train of thought, thinking just how much I want to touch those lips."

She pursed her lips out. "Fine! Touch them then. But kiss me after."

I reached out and brushed her soft, parted lips with my fingers. I could feel my breath growing heavy. Her long, slow sigh was a green light for me.

"Come on." I pulled her back inside toward the counter.

"Wait! We're hanging this up!" She wedged the to-do list on the back wall, front and center.

"Up you go too!" I grabbed her hips and set her on the countertop, and we both began to quickly get her scrubs off. I unbuttoned my pants before I realized I didn't have a rubber. "Well, shit. I'm just not ever prepared for anything! I don't have a condom. I'm sorry!"

"Already on it," she said as she grabbed a condom from her purse.

"Wow, you really are on top of things!"

"I'm about to be on top of things." She licked her lips.

"Not before I finish what I started last night," I growled.

I leaned down and gently spread her apart as I tasted every sweet bit of her. She arched her back and moaned while I traced my name with my tongue along her clit. *J-A-S-O-N* and again and again. I stroked my hard cock while she bucked against my face.

*J-A-S-O—*

"Jason!"

I abruptly pulled my head up. *How the fuck did she know my little trick?*

"Jason! Stop! Fuck! Oh my gosh! I'm on fire. Fuck. Fuck!"

"What? What happ—"

And that was when I felt it. Penis ablaze. Also, fire all over my cheeks and lips, my fingers, and somehow my rib cage. That was weird.

"Holy shitballs! My dick!"

"I need a paper towel! My biscuits are burnin'! My biscuits are burnin'!" She hopped down from the counter and waddled over toward a sink.

I didn't know how I was going to tell her I didn't have the water turned on yet. I was too busy clutching my dick with my jalapeño hands and making it even worse.

"No … water …" I managed to squeak out while I squeezed what little life was left in my little man, fanning it and hopping around like I'd just been bitten … by a fucking hot chicken—on the dick.

"Oh no!" She fanned herself and leaned down to try to blow between her legs.

She was surprisingly pretty flexible. I wondered if she did yoga.

"Do we have any water left? I drank all mine! Did you?" She skipped around, still frantically fanning herself.

I wasn't sure if her pussy was blushing pink from my tongue or from being inflamed. I decided both.

"Hold on! I got one in my truck! Stay put. I'll put out the fire in the hole!"

I'd stuffed my achy snake back in my pants and hobbled to the door. When I got back with the water, Liz looked as if she were in labor. She bent over the counter, slowly rocking back and forth, pants still down, and breathing heavy. If I wasn't on fire myself, I might have been turned on. My cock jumped a little. I guessed I was still turned on even if my balls were about to melt off.

"Here! Put it on a napkin and shove it up there! Let me help!" I doused the napkin with water before she grabbed it from me and held it to her crotch with a loud and almost-orgasmic sigh of relief.

"Ahh—"

I was pretty sure I'd heard a sizzle.

I wet the other napkin and wrapped my willy like a bandage. Now, I had a burned and useless arm and a burned and useless cock.

"Are you okay? I'm so damn sorry, Liz. I had no idea that would happen." I hung my head in shame.

"That had to be the hottest sex I'd ever had!" She laughed. "I mean, you literally gave me fire crotch. It's like you took a chili pepper and planted it right there in between my lips."

"My lips too! And cheeks. And dick. I think it might fall off any second now. I couldn't help but touch it when I was facedown in you. You tasted … so damn good, and I just—" I growled before a fresh wave of heat flushed through my cock and sent it shriveling back into hiding.

Liz was still laughing with each wince I gave, which made her wince and me laugh again until we were both in a fit of giggles and pain.

"Think it's okay? You're the nurse. Should I go get some of that burn cream?"

"No! Don't touch it. It will be fine. It just needs to wear off. It will—shortly, I hope." She hobbled over to me and smiled. "I need to kiss those spicy lips of yours before I go. I'm going to be late if I don't leave now."

"I don't want you to have flaming lips now, too, though!"

"It's worth it." She leaned in and pressed her mouth against mine.

Our bodies both instantly relaxed into a puddle of heat—stupid hot-chicken heat.

"Two for two now. One disaster after another. How about that pizza and dancing Friday? I'll make it up to you, I promise."

"All you have to say is pizza, and I'm there!"

"All right. Pizza."

"See you Friday!"

I watched her turn to leave. There wasn't a pep in her step this time. Just a cringe and a hop as she grabbed her crotch and ran out the door.

# 7

## LIZ

I never knew time could pass by as slow as it had when I was waiting on my date with the famous Jason Jones. All week, since we'd burned our bits in his coffee shop, I had waited like a giggly schoolgirl. My coworkers had even commented on my sudden upbeat mood. They didn't know I was dating a married man, and I wasn't about to tell them. No one would understand. He wasn't really married anymore anyway. How could you divorce someone who had stopped existing?

*"You've got some major rose-colored glasses on, and I'm gonna need you to take them off," Jess said one day over lunch.*

*"What would I do that for? These glasses are the shit! Look at me. I'm dazzling in them. Work it, baby!" I made a duck face and struck a pose.*

*Jess shook her head and stared at me, clearly unamused.*

*"Because you were on a mission to find more out about his wife who disappeared, and now, your judgment is being thrown off because of the feels."*

*"I've given up on the wife thing. I don't care anymore. She's gone, and I know he obviously was hurting for her, but—"*

*"But what? You think you can save him?"*

*"No. I mean, yes. Maybe."*

*"You don't think this is a rebound, do you? Why hasn't he started on divorce papers?"*

*"No! What I feel with him is real, and I'm pretty sure he feels the same way. If he didn't, he wouldn't be trying to make up for these disastrous dates we had. I don't want to seem too pushy, too quick."*

*"Look, I'm just saying, please, if you won't take your rose glasses off, just at least lower them a bit. Before you get hurt. He's still got closure he needs, and I know you think you'll provide that for him—and maybe you will! I hope you will. But he's still married, and he's yet to figure out how to ... not be. So, be careful."*

*"Yes, Mama Jess. Cross my heart—again."*

That little exchange had been two days ago, and now, with tonight being the big night, I was on the edge of an emotional roller coaster.

*What do I wear?*

*Should I dress to impress or cover my butt, so I can shake it on the dance floor?*

*Will he think I'm a ho if I twerk?*

*Should I pack a toothbrush?*

*Are we finally going to do it tonight?*

*And if so, where? Am I going to his place, or is he coming here?*

My mind raced as I made myself ready for my big date.

"Mr. Jones, eat your heart out!" I said to myself in the mirror. "Self, you got this!"

I tossed my hair and checked my nails, like the diva I hoped I looked like. I needed Jason to sing in my ear. He could sing about how amazing he found me. How utterly incredible I was and how he was falling so hard for me and about how he was so lucky that I was here now and ... *Kate who? Kate what?*

I over-spritzed myself with perfume and headed out the door. Jess and Luke were dropping me off tonight at the brewery where I planned on meeting Jason. He'd offered to pick me up, but I told him I wouldn't be driving anyway. I was about to get lit. It had been a while ... well, like, a week or something.

"Oh, wow! Look at you!" Luke beamed from the driver's seat as I catwalked to the car.

"You're wearing your come-fuck-me heels again," Jess pointed out.

"Duh. It's Jason Jones! By the way, he plays next week at that one place you told me about. Blue Lights or something? Can we go see him? Please, please, please? Luke can meet him, too, then." I gave them my best puppy-dog eyes.

Luke grabbed Jess's hand and smiled. "Is that right? So, this Jason character ... is he really all he's cracked up to be? Do I really need to meet him, so I can swoon over him too?"

"I hate to admit it, but yes. He is. He will set your drawers on fire. Literally. Ask Liz," Jess replied.

Luke raised his eyebrows. She had obviously not yet told him about the chicken incident—surprisingly.

I sighed. "It was hot—in every way imaginable. Finger-lickin' hot!"

"Oh, well, count me in then! Mr. Jones sounds so … dreamy," he teased.

"I see she at least told you about the Mr. Jones thing then," I said.

"Oh, well, how could I not? It was hot! Plus, it gave me some ideas." Jess laughed and winked at her husband.

"You bet it did! I owe you a thanks, Liz." Luke caught my eye in the rearview mirror and smiled as wide as I'd ever seen him smile.

"You two are ridiculous!" I shook my head in mock disbelief and maybe a little bit of jealousy. I hoped I could one day have a long-term relationship as spicy as that—without hot chicken.

My breath caught in my chest as soon as I spotted him at the entrance to the restaurant. I drank him in slowly before he noticed me. His sexy and disheveled hair, his cut-just-right jeans, and his fitted T-shirt. And his biceps, biceps, and biceps. I would never get over his biceps. Every time I saw them flex, I felt myself flex too—in my pants. I was a walking Kegel machine when he was around.

*Squeeze and squeeze and squeeze and squeeze.*

"There's my sunshine!" He smiled as he reached for my hand and pulled me in for a quick kiss.

*Squeeze and squeeze …*

"Hey you." I was already breathless.

"You look fabulous, as always." He stood back, admiring me as I pushed my hip out and struck a pose. "And damn, I love your attitude." He laughed.

"I'm glad you do. I'm a fireball of fun. I'll show you tonight."

"Oh, I hope you do."

I really hoped I could show him some fun tonight. I was just a teeny, tiny bit nervous. After all, he had been the one with the spankings. He clearly had more experience in this area than I did. I'd had plenty of experience, probably more so than I'd ever admit—to myself or anyone else—but I just hadn't had the Jason Jones experience … the wild and crazy, *spank my ass*, and *pull my hair* stuff. Maybe once or twice. Probably eight times. Wow, I was a big whore. But those men didn't count because they weren't Jason Jones. They didn't have the charisma *my* Mr. Jones had.

"It smells amazing in here," I said as I scooted my way across a booth.

Pizza and booze were definitely how you could hit me in the feels.

"It's one of my favorite places. I'm a bit biased though, as this is the first place I ever performed. I still do every now and then."

"Is that right? The famous Jason Jones started right here? I'm sitting in history then!"

"Hardly famous. I'm not selling records or even playing regular gigs—yet."

"I'd say, by the way all of these women stare at you, you're pretty famous. I think they know who you are."

A very young, very blonde, and very busty waitress bounced over to our table. She parted her lips in a round little O and cooed, "What can I get you, Mr. Jones?"

*Mr. Jones. Cooo.*

"Oh, hey there, Tammy. I think we're going to probably start off with some cocktails."

"The usual?" She fluttered her eyes.

I wondered if he had spanked *Tammy* too.

*Cooo.*

"Let's try something new today. How about it, Liz? See anything you like?"

I only had a moment to glance over the menu before deciding on something strong—a cocktail made with Memphis vodka. I'd been to Memphis plenty of times, and with my eyes boob-level to Tammy, I was feeling very Memphis-ish.

"I'll have whatever she is having." He nodded, watching my eyebrows fight to keep level. I wasn't sure if I wanted to raise them or narrow them at him.

Tammy fluttered her eyes and left.

"What?" He grinned at me.

"Nothing, nothing … *Mr. Jones.*"

"Aha! I thought you'd caught on to that. Well, it's not like that. Never has been."

"I told you, you're famous already. You're sexy as fuck *and* talented. You could have any girl you want."

"I just want one." He looked at me with an expression as serious as I'd ever seen on him.

I felt a blush move through my body and settle on my cheeks. Or was that a hot flash? He made me break a sweat. I cleared my throat and my thoughts, and I changed the subject. I couldn't jump into a relationship with a married but maybe-not-technically-married man, could I? No matter how much I wanted to date Jason, there was still Kate to worry about. I needed to see some progress in that area of his life before I let myself fall even more.

"All right, Jason. Now, we are going to part ways with what comes next."

"Uh-oh. What comes next?"

"Pizza. What kind do you like? On the count of three, we name our top five toppings. Ready?"

"Oh boy ..."

"One. Two. Three," I said, followed by, "Peppers, onions, mushrooms, pineapple, olives—black."

"Sausage, pepperoni, bacon, ham, jalapeños!"

"Egads! You're a walking coronary waiting to happen!" I touched my hand to my heart. I found our fatal flaw.

"I don't like vegetables."

"And you, sir, are what is wrong with this world."

"Well, only potatoes. You know, the fried ones. French fries."

He sat back and took a long sip of one of the cocktails that Tammy had oh-so happily bounced over. Her curls bounced in sync with her boobies. Her ass hopped along behind her.

*Cooo.*

"I knew this was too good to be true. Oh well! Better call it quits now. This is a deal-breaker for me," I said. I actually felt a tiny bit of relief that we didn't have everything in common. Things had been *too* perfect, which, in my experience, always meant that it wasn't real and it wouldn't last.

"Hey, wait! I've got a brilliant idea!" He reached over the table and covered my hands with his.

There went that electric energy again. It coursed right through my fingers and down and out of my toes. It only stopped to tingle between my legs.

*Squeeze and squeeze and squeeze.*

If he kept touching me like that, I was going to be able to shoot ping-pong balls clear across the room with my vag muscles alone. That would be an interesting side hustle.

"Is your brilliant idea that you'll get your cholesterol checked?"

"Well, no. Do you think I need to?"

"Probably."

"Will it hurt? I have a thing about needles." He shivered and crossed his arms.

I saw goose bumps on his flesh from across the table.

"You have tattoos! How can you be afraid of a needle?"

"That's different!"

"Oh my goodness. No, it's not! A cholesterol check is just a prick."

"Will you be the one doing the pricking?"

"I'll give you a big prick if you deny me olives on my pizza," I said as I pinched his arm to give him an example of what he would have coming to him.

"Yikes! My naughty nurse! I won't deny you the olives. But I was going to say, let's order individual pizzas and keep this a happy relationship. I can compromise. I get my meat, and you get your rabbit food. See how easy I can be?"

"Deal. But I do need some mozzarella sticks, and I don't like to share my sauce."

"Now, we're talking!"

I told Jason to go ahead and order our food while I made a quick trip to the ladies' room. I felt his eyes on my ass as I walked away, swaying to the beat of Toto's "Africa." The singer onstage was hot as fuck, and I was pretty sure I caught his eyes following me as well.

What was it with me and men who could sing *and* play guitar? If every man invested in those skills, they'd have a bed full of women.

"Oh, sorry!" Tammy bumped into me as I opened the door to the restroom. Her jiggly bits jiggled again.

"Oops! Didn't see you there!" I sidestepped her ample Jell-O chest and made my way toward the sink.

"You're here with Mr. Jones, right?"

*Mr. Jones. Cooo.*

"I am," I replied.

"Is he okay now?"

"What do you mean?"

"Did he find Kate?"

"Oh."

I started to get agitated with all of this Kate business. It was as if I couldn't escape the ghost wife, or ex-wife, or whatever she had been.

*Mythological creature maybe?*

"He was pretty torn up over it. I just thought, maybe you'd know more since he's here with *you*. I guess he is over her, is all. Did he ever find her?"

"No, he didn't."

I kept my answer short and sweet, partly because I had no idea if he was over her and partly because, *What the fuck?* I grew more and more uncomfortable. Of course I wanted to tell her, *Hell yes, he is over Kate because he is with me, duh!* But I played nice and kept my mouth shut, which she wasn't making it easy for me to do.

"That's a shame. She is such a nice girl. He always gushed over her. I didn't think he would ever be able to recover. It's good to see he is back on the market."

*Back on the market? Did she hope for a chance at Mr. Jones? Well, tough titty! Tough, jiggly Tammy titty! Cooo.*

"What makes you think he is back on the market?" I stared in the mirror at her reflection behind me. Damn, that Memphis vodka had worked fast on my already-feisty attitude. Ayesha was about to show her claws.

"Is he?"

"That is a really great question to ask—him."

"Okay!" She bounced out the door, quickly followed by me. Her legs scurried across the floor so fast that I could barely even keep up.

*Is she trying to out-bounce me? Is this a bounce-off?*

I shimmied up beside her, making my bits jiggle for Jason, too, as we raced toward him. We were practically elbow to elbow. If I did a quick right jab, I would be able to knock her off course. But I was curious about Jason's answer to her question. Was he on the market? And if he said yes, what did that mean for me?

"Jason! Hi. Sorry about the wait! I ran into your … date … and she told me that you never heard from Kate. I'm so sorry!" Tammy said, smoothing her apron. She was out of breath from the race and also because her knockers looked heavy … and suffocating.

"Actually, she asked about Kate. I just told her no, you never found her. She was interested if you were available and on the market, is what I think she was trying to say," I said as I scooted into the booth in front of him.

Tammy's cheeks blushed pink. Her jiggly bits suddenly stopped jiggling. Poor thing.

"I, uh … what? No, no, I never found Kate." He shook his head at both of us.

We stared back, waiting for him to answer if he was available or not.

"Oh, well," he continued, "I'm not available. I'm a one-woman guy, loyal to the core, despite my marital status or un-status, obviously. I'm with Liz." He smiled at me.

*"I'm with Liz," he said. Liz! That's me! Fuck yes. Bounce on out of here, Tammy! Cooo.*

"Congratulations on getting back out there. It's so good to see that you are over what all happened—with Kate. Now, what can I order for you?" Tammy took out her pen and waited on our order.

Jason, being the gentleman he was, politely told her what we wanted and sent her on her merry way.

"What was that all about?" I asked.

"Ugh, sorry. I should have told you. She is friends with Kate. They had just become friends right before Kate disappeared. Not good friends, but Tammy's the kind of friend who wants to fuck your man. She sent out a lot of signals, but like I said, never happened. Anyway, that's my take on it."

"Wow! Yikes! Did you really mean that loyalty and exclusivity and all? I'm not expecting anything from you. I just didn't know if you were playing the field or—"

He leaned across the table and took my chin in his hand, slightly brushing my lips with his thumb before he kissed me.

*Squeeze and squeeze.*

"I mean that. I like you. A lot. I'm not interested in playing the field. I'm interested in playing with you. No games. I don't need games. I got my prize."

"You sure do have a way with words. Maybe put that line in a song."

"I like the way you think."

"Well, right now, I'm thinking Tammy might poison our food."

"Maybe just yours." He laughed.

Surprisingly, I did not roll over and die after I ate my pizza. Tammy disappeared into the night, and our new waitress was much less bouncy and much more friendly, and not the *hey, I want to fuck your boyfriend* friendly. She was more of a *hey, I am going to get you some extra sauce for those cheese sticks* friendly.

*The night is salvaged! I might actually get laid tonight,* I thought as we left the restaurant and headed out to dance off our pizza calories.

The time had come for me to shine. Not only were my pizza-eating skills impressive, but I could shake it like a saltshaker too. I often fantasized about putting on a striptease for my man, except there was always one problem. I never had a man ... not a steady one anyway. I'd dated but never settled. Probably because I refused to settle. Commitment issues and all. There hadn't been anyone good enough for me until I met Jason. And even then, there was the third wheel—his nonexistent wife. But, according to our pizza-shop conversation, she was headed out of the picture.

*"I'm with Liz."* His voice echoed in my thoughts as we walked down Broadway Street.

"Where are you taking me?" He gripped my hand as I weaved in and out of the crowds.

"Somewhere to dance. My *favorite* place to dance. No line-dancing, but I think you'll like it."

"Oh! Good! Because I don't know any line dances anyway."

"Me either! It's not really my thing."

"What is your thing?"

"You'll see."

We stopped in front of the bar. Not just the bar, but *the* bar—Whiskey Row. It looked and smelled like ... *college.*

"I know this bar," he said. "It looks like tonight will be full of trouble."

"It'd better be! Follow me," I called loudly as we made our way through the crowded entry.

I'd been to Whiskey Row several times. It was my go-to when I needed to dance it out—or you know, get jiggy with it with some hot strangers. The crowd here was different than the normal crowds on Broadway. There was a lot less boot-scootin' and a lot more booty-poppin', which I was particularly good at.

Jess, my usual dance partner, on the other hand, was a head-bobber. I'd tried to teach her several times how to shake it, but the only thing she could do was stand like a bobblehead and awkwardly sway her hips like she was trying to pick a wedgie without using her hands. That was, until she had tequila—which, remember, we didn't go there anymore. Some clothes might have come off that night because I never found my bra. It was probably hanging up somewhere in the men's restroom.

I double-checked behind me to make sure Jason wasn't lost in the sea of humping we bounced through. If he wasn't with me, I might have not-so-accidentally gotten lost in there too. But alas, it was showtime. I grabbed his hand and led him up the stairs. The music, or my heart, was pounding in my chest. I was about to get down or go down—quickly and in cardiac arrest. I wondered if this place had an AED machine.

Jason muttered something in my ear, but the music was so obnoxiously loud that I couldn't hear him.

*Something, something, pet my hamster?*

No, that couldn't be right.

*Something, something, something dancer?*

I gave up trying to decipher his words and pushed him further and further onto the dance floor. He flashed me a mischievous look.

The lights suddenly flashed brighter, and the bass dropped low—just like my ass. I couldn't help it. That always happened when I heard a beat I could dance to. It didn't matter if I was in the middle of Walmart, the dentist office, or at work; I was going to dance. Okay, maybe not like this. This was just slutty. But I needed Jason drooling. I was finally going to get pinned against that wall tonight, damn it!

"How am I supposed to keep up with you? My white-boy moves can't do you justice!" he shouted over the music.

"Sorry, sorry. I was feeling the beat. Okay, I'll take it down a notch. Just grind on me. You can do that, can't you, Mr. Jones?"

He grinned as he placed his hands on my ribs and turned me around to face the crowd. He grabbed my waist and pulled me into him, gyrating his hips into my ass. The music thumped harder, and so did he. I felt the firmness in his pants as I pushed myself into him. Cock to ass, ass to cock. It was hot—too hot. I felt my back start to sweat as we rubbed against each other.

I closed my eyes and let myself go to the music. Our bodies moved together as we found our perfect rhythm. If we could have sex on the dance floor, we would because these moves were basically the same we'd done in his changing room at the bar. We worked so well together, at everything. Peas and carrots. Peaches and cream. Wine and cheese. I was beginning to see how compatible we really were. Any man who could hold his own on the dance floor with me, the booty-poppin'-on-a-handstand professional, was a man who could handle me. I hadn't found those often—if ever.

*Thump, thump, thump* went the music, and *thump, thump, thump* went his stiff cock against me. Also, *thump, thump, thump* went my heart. That couldn't be good. I was out of breath but not out of shape. That could only mean one thing—the feels. I was falling for Jason even more, just like I had told myself I wouldn't do.

*Gosh damn it, Jason, and your moves like Jagger!*

"Do you want a drink?" He leaned down to talk in my ear so that I could hear him over the crowd.

Just the feel of his breath on my skin made me even more wiggly and breathless.

"No. Not yet. I want to stay here."

The music slowed into something much more sensual, like Marvin Gaye sensual, like I needed to be dipped à la *Dirty Dancing*-style and then passionately kissed while everyone formed a circle around us, cheering us on. Yes, that was what this night needed.

I turned to face him, and this time, I pulled him into me. I still felt him through his jeans. He was as hard as a rock—a really, really hard rock. Fucking granite even. I wondered if he had taken a dick pill. I never felt anything so hard in my life. He was going to spearhead me with that thing if he kept pointing it at me. But I guessed I would die a happy woman at least.

We swayed back and forth to the music with our arms tightly wrapped around one another. I closed my eyes and rested my head against his chest. I could feel his heartbeat against my cheek. I wanted to remember this forever. This would be one of those memories I'd mentally file away and take out when all the world went to shit. But really, with Jason, I didn't think the world could go to shit. He lit up everything. My heart, my soul, my brain, my pants.

I was lost in the moment when I looked up at him and caught his eye. He had a familiar look on his face. It was the same dreamy expression he'd had when he first told me about Kate. In an instant, his lips were on mine, breathing life into me—like a dementor, but in reverse. He breathed his soul into me. All those sweet melodies, warm touches, and electric sparks. I felt the butterflies rise up in my stomach as he kissed me right there in front of everyone. He tasted of want, need, desire, and also maybe a little bit of meaty pizza.

*Thump, thump, thump.*
*Squeeze and squeeze.*

# JASON

I couldn't believe Liz was coming to my home even if that had been my plan all along.

It was like the advice my dad had given me. "Wish in one hand and shit in the other. Then, see which one fills up the fastest."

I'd really wished she would stay with me, but I hadn't actually thought it would happen. And now, it was happening, and now, I was freaking out.

I still wasn't sure how we had gotten from point A to point B. Point A being us about to hump each other on the dance floor and point B being my place. All I knew was that she had taken one look at me and was all over me like stink on shit, which was another great euphemism from my dear old dad. You'd think we'd had some type of terrible obsession with bathroom humor in my house. We had … which brought me to Deuce.

I had taken Deuce to the groomer yesterday, so he would look as spiffy as a dog with missing teeth and half an ear could. When I had adopted him from the shelter years ago, they'd given me such a sad story that I couldn't even repeat it. So, now, when people asked me what was wrong with his face, I just told them it was a bad bar fight and that they should see the other dog. In reality, Deuce wasn't tough at all. Remember how he had let that crazy redhead in my house?

I wasn't only worried about Deuce. I was also terrified my house wouldn't be up to snuff for the extra, extra Liz. I had cleaned for ten straight hours yesterday. I'd never done that in my life. Not that I was messy, but I was a man after all. I sometimes didn't see that a shoe had been left on the floor for two weeks. My mind just didn't work that way. Except yesterday, it had. I'd even washed floorboards.

"Wow, you really are far! It's beautiful out here though. So peaceful. I can see all the stars! You don't see stars like this at my house!" Liz said as we hopped out of my truck.

"Yep. It's very, very peaceful." I put my hands in my pockets to slyly wipe the sweat off of my palms.

"Look, look! There's a lightning bug! Oh! And another one!" She pointed toward the huge field that was my front yard.

I smiled at her excitement. It made me excited too. Of course I saw lightning bugs all the time but not through Liz's eyes.

"Wanna catch some?" I asked.

"Can we?"

"Go on ahead and see if you can. I'll get a jar."

Liz squealed as she ran off into the dark. I watched her disappear and quickly snuck away to my garage. I hadn't even thought about cleaning that part of my house. I never parked my truck in there anyway because, well, I couldn't. My garage was packed full of shit. The same shit I had carried around for years and never found the time to go through. No way was Liz going to see my dirty little secret of laziness.

I hopped over boxes of who knew what and made my way toward a shelf full of crap. Kate used to be into canning stuff at one point, so I knew I had to have some jars around here somewhere.

"I got one, Jason!" I heard from the front as I found a jar, grabbed it, and jumped through the obstacle course, quickly shutting the garage before she could find me.

"Let's see it!" I raced toward her.

"Look," she said, holding her cupped hands out.

I peeked between her fingers and saw a dim, flashing glow.

"Here. Let's put him in here. I see more of them out there. We'll get him some friends!"

I helped Liz gently put the lightning bug into the jar, and I carried it to the porch. She ran off and back again, cradling another before I had a chance to catch up. I followed her back out into the field and chased after my own bug.

"How are you finding them so fast?" I called out to her, pausing to catch my breath.

Running was not my thing, nor was any other exercise aside from pounding weights for these biceps that Liz loved to get her hands on. This week alone, I'd increased my lifts by a few pounds.

"Ha! You want me to tell you my secrets? Why? Are you trying to make this into some sort of competition?"

"No!" I lied.

She scoffed at me and ran off into the dark. Her familiar peaches-and-cream scent hung in the air around me, intoxicating me into a drunken lust. Oh, how I wanted her dripping for me again. My tongue on that sweet, velvet pussy of hers was my favorite new hobby.

"Three to zero!" she yelled, breaking my trance.

*Game on.*

I rushed to the other side of the field in a sudden fit of determination to win not only this countrified competition, but to also win my lady's heart—and maybe her body too. We still hadn't had sex since that first night at the bar. Shit had just kept happening, but tonight, Liz was mine.

I caught up to her, finding three, four, seven lightning bugs of my own. At this point, the jar lit up like a tiny disco.

"What the hell?" she said as she sat down on the porch and looked into the jar. "How did you catch all of these?"

"You think I've lived out here all of these years and never learned to catch a firefly?" I asked.

I hadn't. This was actually a first for me, but I couldn't tell her the truth. I couldn't tell her that the scent of her, the looks of her, the feel of her all enticed me into a lust-drunk stupor. And I couldn't tell her that I was willing to do anything to win her over tonight and always.

"You're good." She turned the jar around in her palms, peering inside of it.

"It's for you. You're very own jar of stars. I want you to take it home with you, and tomorrow night, you can let them go at your place. So, you'll have a part of my starry night sky with you. We have to poke holes in the lid and put a damp paper towel and some grass in there. But they should be okay for one day."

"So, you want me to go home tomorrow?" She pulled out a few blades of grass and tucked them into the jar.

"Yes … tomorrow. Stay with me tonight."

"Do you mean that? You really want me to?"

"Of course I do. I already bought you a toothbrush. It's pink with sparkles."

She reached over and kissed me. Her mouth parted into a smile I felt with my lips. Her tongue slowly traced along my bottom lip, and I instantly stiffened.

"Thank you for my stars, Jason. *When he shall die, take him and cut him out into stars, and he shall make the face of heaven so fine that all the world will be in love with night and pay no worship to the garish sun.* Shakespeare."

"That is beautiful, except for the cutting-him-up part. But I'll let it slide, knowing you're a redhead and all. It could probably be worse. I didn't know you were a Shakespeare fan, though I did notice when I picked you up on our first date that you had an eclectic choice of books on your coffee table."

"There's a lot you don't know about me, but yes, I'm a total book nerd."

"Any favorite authors? Anyone I might have heard of? I'll admit, it's been a while since I've touched a book."

"Well, we are gonna have to fix that! Klara Woods is a favorite of mine right now. She's relatively new, but oh-so good. Sexy, steamy stuff. I'll have to read it to you in bed. Also, she's a local Tennessee gal, so she knows what she is doing."

"Is that so? Steamy in Tennessee. Sounds like a plan."

"Let's do this plan."

"Come on." I took her hand and pulled her up and into me, kissing her mouth again. That sweet taste of her was addicting. "Let me show you around first. I also need to introduce you to someone."

"Oh?"

I caught the hesitation in her voice. Maybe she thought I had a secret child—or worse, Kate was back.

"It's a dog, just a dog," I answered a little too quickly. "My dog. He's a bit of a nuisance. He still pees when he is excited and greeting people, so I'll let him run out to greet you here, in the grass, where he can pee all he wants."

I opened the door to let Deuce out. He was waiting patiently with his half-crooked grin, a puddle of drool collecting underneath him. He hobbled out the door and ran straight toward Liz, his pee spraying everywhere.

"Oh my gosh! What a cute little thing!"

Deuce excitedly peed out every ounce that had been in his body before deciding to jump up and wrap himself around Liz's leg in a friendly hug—a humping sort of hug, as in he totally went to town with her knee.

"Damn it, Deuce! That's not how you greet a lady, no matter how much you want to!" I shooed him off of Liz.

"It's okay. I get that a lot."

Liz reached down to pet him as he wagged his nub of a tail so hard that he slipped out a fart. Typical.

"Wow. That's impressive for something so short and fat like you, Deuce!" She rubbed behind his ears as he flopped down and rolled on his back, begging for her to rub his tummy too. "Aww." She laughed.

"So, there ya go. That's my dog, my roommate, my shame—Deuce. He's my derpy little friend who has problems controlling his urges—and his gas."

"I know a lot of men like that! No worries!" She stood up and glanced around my damn-near-immaculate home.

Aside from Deuce, it smelled like rainy meadows in here or spring rain or whatever the hell it was I had picked up and plugged into every socket I could find in hopes of covering up the Deuce stench.

"Your house is really beautiful. It's so cozy and clean in here." She walked around my living room, looking at the old vinyl artwork I had hanging on the walls. "You should put some of these in the coffee shop too. They're great!"

"That's a really good idea! Glad you like it. Here, let me show you my man cave, or ... I guess it couldn't be called a cave since it's outside. Hmm ... my man space. I'm going to take care of those fireflies and grab a drink though first. Would you like one? I make a pretty mean gin and tonic. It's not crafty, but it's classic. Like me."

"Oh, well, how can I resist that? A classic cocktail in Jason Jones's man space." She moved closer to me and ran her index finger from my collarbone down to the button on my jeans, sending my dick into high alert.

*Schwing.*

"Do that again, and we are skipping all this romance stuff and heading straight to bed," I growled in her ear.

I grabbed her hips and pulled her closer. Her breath was heavy already.

"I like the romance stuff. I'll behave but only for a little bit. I'm not sure how much longer I can resist you. Do you have any idea how long I've been waiting to get back into your pants?" She turned her bottom lip down into a pout.

I wanted to take my dick out right then and there and push her up against all that vintage artwork. But I noticed Deuce sat at the door, waiting already. He knew my routines, and I knew his. If I didn't open that door and let him out now, things would get messy. Just another thing to ruin a good date night.

"I'm going to get in those pants of yours and make them mine here soon. Just let me let this dog out real quick before he turns this night around—and not in a good way." I opened the back door, and out he ran. "Come on out. I've got a gas firepit out here I'll light. You can relax, and I'll bring you your drink."

I lit the firepit on low as I watched the excitement spread across her face. The warm glow of the fire flickered in her soft blue eyes. I could stay there forever, watching her smile.

"This just keeps getting better and better! Fireflies, firelight, my own jar of stars. Jason Jones and a farty dog named Deuce. This is perfect. It really is." She settled into an Adirondack chair. "Oh my goodness, and is that bacon I smell?" She moaned. "This is heaven."

*She's a keeper,* I thought. She'd had me at bacon.

"It's the grill behind you, but if you like bacon, I got something for you. Let me grab the cocktails and some snacks. I'll be right back. I think I can make the night even better. Sit back, relax. *Mi casa es su casa.*"

"Snacks. You are still speaking my language, Mr. Jones."

I headed to the kitchen and quickly put together a charcuterie board, just like I knew she liked—crackers, cheese, bacon jam, pickles, blackberries. If I hadn't won her over yet, she certainly would be won over now. And then, even if somehow she wasn't impressed, I always had the guitar. But I thought I was doing good so far. I'd even surprised myself.

*Fuck it, I'm grabbing the guitar and going all in.*

I hadn't scrubbed my house, groomed my dog, shopped at the farmers market, and shaved my balls just to have a ho-hum night with Liz. Tonight, she was mine. I felt butterflies flutter about in my stomach as I thought about her and realized how I'd forgotten what that even felt like.

"Damn!" Her mouth dropped open as she saw my fancy-pants plate of what I would call just cheese and crackers, but for her sake, I called it charcuterie. "You're going to be the best host when you open your shop," she said as I handed her a cocktail and set the food on the table beside her.

"Dig in. I've got to grab one more thing. Oh, and that's bacon jam for all your bacon-y needs."

I heard a primal groan come from her as I ran back inside to get my guitar. I noticed Deuce had already taken up residence at her feet, no doubt waiting on a piece of cheese to drop. I hoped it wouldn't. Cheese did not settle well with him, just like with everything else.

"You're going to give me my own special concert?" she asked as soon as she saw my guitar in hand.

"I am. I told you I needed to make up for our terrible dates."

"I'd say, you have already made up for all of them ten times over, but even with how wonky they turned out, I would still do them all over again."

"Well, Liz, you're something special, and you deserve only the best. So, relax and enjoy the night. Any requests?"

"Something not country."

"I'm on it."

I took a long drink of my cocktail and shot her what I hoped was a panty-melting grin. Even though I knew the effects my singing had on women, I'd only ever played alone for one other woman, and that was Kate. She had liked it well enough, but she'd still had that far-off look in her eyes when I played. She hadn't looked at me all razzle-dazzled like Liz did.

I began to sing my rendition of Prince's "Little Red Corvette" as I watched Liz melt back into her seat. She slowly sipped her cocktail, licking her lips. Before I even finished verse one, she had bedroom eyes. They weren't just bedroom eyes though. She was far beyond that *come hither* look. No, the look she gave me was one that only a redhead could do—not psycho this time, but ravenous. Ravenous for my cock, which, I admitted, made me sing even sultrier.

I belted out the lyrics so loud that even the crickets stopped chirping for a minute. I needed an outlet at the moment for all this passion that had been building up inside me, and right now, that outlet was my voice and my hands. With each stroke of the guitar, I wanted to strum her clit. With each high note I sang, I wanted to make her sing even higher. I glanced over at her and could see she felt the same. She fished out an ice cube and ran it along her collarbone.

*Fuck.*

I lost my train of thought and quit singing.

"Sorry!" She giggled. "I didn't mean to interrupt. I was just getting so damn hot. You do that to me."

"I think it's this fire!"

"Maybe, but it's definitely you and that guitar of yours too. Can you teach me? Please, Mr. Jones?"

I felt my cock come alive as soon as she muttered the word *please*.

"You want me to teach you how to play? Sure, I can do that. Or I can try. I'm not the best teacher, but I'm sure I can show you some things." I winked. "Let's get away from the fire though. You're right; it is hot. Come sit over here. I'll grab a blanket."

I tiptoed around the sleeping Deuce, who suddenly decided to wake up and be a part of our blanket gang. He followed me inside and back out while I quietly explained to him what wasn't going to happen. He was not supposed to drool anymore, hump anymore, and certainly not let any more obnoxious smells out, or else he would be put inside.

He cocked his head to the side. He knew I meant business.

I laid the blanket on the stone patio, close enough to see the fire, but not close enough to make me sweat, which was what I would be doing if I was going to teach her how to play—my way.

"Come on over here, gorgeous, and sit," I said.

I let her get comfortable before I scooted in behind her with my chest pressed against her back as she cradled my baby—my guitar.

"You put this hand here, and then this one goes down here." I moved her hands in place to show her how to begin.

"Then what?" She looked back at me.

"Then … well … you sing. And strum the guitar, of course." I nodded for her to begin.

"What shall I sing?"

"Whatever comes to mind."

*"Deuce is really stinky right now."*

"You want to write a stinky Deuce song? I think we can manage that."

"Let's do it."

"Okay. Hope this doesn't get too awkward."

"Bring it."

Deuce lay down at our feet and looked at us patiently, as if he knew we were talking about him.

*Cockblocker.*

I brought my arms around her and put them on the guitar. *Here goes nothing,* I thought. *So much for a romantic evening.*

*"Stinky Deuce, Stinky Deuce, what are they feeding you?"*

"That's cheating!" Liz laughed.

"Fine! Let's see …"

# NASHVEGAS NIGHTS

I strummed the guitar with her hands. It sounded terrible, but it would have to do.

*I can't se-Deuce you tonight.*
*My dog's smell just ain't right.*
*And he refuses to just leave us be.*

*But if you and I*
*Can sneak back inside,*
*I promise I'll set your mind free …*
*Of all these foul smells*
*Coming from my dear dog.*

*It's terrible.*
*I'm sorry.*
*I know.*
*But if you give me just one chance*
*After that sexy dance*
*When we almost fucked*
*On the dance floor.*

*No, I can't se-Deuce you tonight.*
*But just know I'll still try.*

*After this damn dog falls asleep,*
*Let's turn this fire off*
*And head back inside.*
*I hope you're ready,*
*As I'll be going in deep.*

*See you later, Deuce,*
*You little cockblock.*
*May your rotten-ass gas go away.*
*Your ugly mug*
*is scaring sweet Liz,*
*And now, she won't want to stay!*

"He does not scare me! That poor thing!" She reached over to pat Deuce on the head.

He leaned into her and drooled.

I had to admit, he had been pretty good tonight, aside from his farting problem. But I guessed he couldn't really help with that issue, being a dog and all. At least he hadn't humped her leg again—yet. I wasn't even going to go there with a song.

"Can I try? I think I have something else on my mind now. Even if I still smell Deuce."

"By all means, the guitar is yours. Strum away, sweet thing."

She took a deep breath and started. I could hear the quiver in her voice. It was cute how nervous she was.

*Ja-ja-ja-ja-jay-son,*
*I'm yours for the ta-ta-ta-ta-take-in'.*
*You don't need to se-du-ooo-ooo-ooo-ooo-ce me.*
*I'm yours, so just please u-ooo-oooo-ooo-use me.*

She turned to proudly look back at me. I was putty in her hands. I closed my eyes and breathed in her breaths for as long as I could before I had to feel her lips on mine. She let out a little sigh of relief as soon as I pushed my mouth onto hers.

"Well, how did I do?" she said as soon as we came up for air.

"No one's ever sang to me before. Now, I get it. My boxers are melting." I hopped up and rested the guitar on the table.

"Really? I'm that good, eh?"

I reached down and picked her up in my arms, carrying her inside. She threw her arms around my neck and laughed. Deuce followed behind us.

"And now, you get to see my bedroom." I kicked in the door to my room and walked her to the bed before I threw her down on it—not so gently.

Her breathing was already ragged.

I ran back to the door and shut it before Deuce could hobble his stocky ass in to follow us. He was not going to mess this up for me. I couldn't put on my best moves with him watching, drooling, and farting.

*Sorry, little cockblocker.*

We both began to strip our clothes off, throwing them this way and that. She successfully threw her panties on top of my head.

"Ha-haha-haha! I meant to throw them past you, but that will work too!" She laughed.

I grabbed them from my head, closed my eyes, put them to my nose, and breathed them in before I even had a chance to think about what I was doing. A primal feeling overtook me, and I needed her, all of her all over all of me.

"Fuck, that was hot," she said, watching me.

I dived into the bed. "Come here." The sweet scent of her had me ravenous to taste her. "I want you on my face. I need you straddling my mouth. I so fucking need that. I want to taste you, to breathe you in, to swirl my tongue inside that tight, juicy pussy of yours."

She gasped as she swung her leg over my head, and I pulled her hips onto my face. Her hands gripped the back of the headboard as she rocked back and forth. I couldn't see much of anything from my point of view, but I was sure her head was tossed back and her eyes were closed as she fucked my face. I started to tug on my cock while she rode my face.

"Wait! Let me." She turned around and lowered herself down on me. This time, bending over and taking my dick in her mouth while she wiggled her hips against my lips.

"Fucking hell, Liz," I muttered into her pussy as I put my arms around her and tightly squeezed her into me, closer. I didn't even care if she suffocated me at this point; it would be worth it.

Her tongue circled around the tip before she took me all in. One of her hands reached over and grasped the bed, steadying herself, and the other grabbed my cock, stroking it in rhythm to her slow-sucking mouth. I felt her forget to breathe as she took me in deep, the head of my dick touching the back of her throat.

I sucked her clit back into my mouth and thrust my hips forward as she moaned like I was the best damn ice cream cone she'd ever tasted, and I hoped I was because, for days, I had been drinking a shit-ton of pineapple juice to sweeten my sauce, so to speak. When I'd said I had done a lot of planning for this, I meant it.

"I can't hang on much longer, Jason. I'm— I'm—"

Her thighs trembled as she put her mouth back on me. Her rhythm became fast and needy. I wasn't about to finish before I got her wrapped around me again.

"I need to be inside you." I turned my head and growled into her thigh. My hand fumbled next to me where I had conveniently laid a row of condoms. I'd told ya, prep work.

She saw me, stopped what she was doing, and crawled down my body. She ripped the condom open with her teeth, threw the wrapper over her shoulder, and lowered herself on me—backward.

*Fucking fuck, fuck, fucksticks.*

I ached to explode. I tried everything I could to hold back as I watched her sweet ass bounce on me. It had to feel like she was riding a bolt of lightning, which she loved because she cried out louder and louder as I forced myself up and she forced herself down. I wasn't surprised that I saw sparks a time or two each time we clashed.

"Say my name," she said, breathless.

"What?" I wasn't sure I'd heard her right. All this bouncing made my mind boggled.

"Mr. Jones, I need you to say my name while I fuck this hard cock of yours. You like that, don't you?" she growled through her teeth as she roughly ground on me.

*So, she wants to play that game, does she?*

"What's your last name? Quick! I'm about to burst!" I bore down to try to stop my flow of what was surely about to shoot out of me like water out of a fire hydrant—forceful as fuck.

She stopped.

*No, no, no.*

"Are you okay? Something wrong?" I sat up on my elbows, still throbbing away inside her.

"It's my real name. I don't want you to say it. Just say Liz." She looked back at me.

I nodded hurriedly, ready to get back to our game. *Giddy up.*

"Fuck me, Liz. You dirty girl. *My* dirty girl." I slapped her ass hard as she started to bounce again.

"Mmm, Mr. Jones!"

She reached around and started to rub herself as she rocked on my cock. Her bottom gyrated me into being hypnotized by … Liz because, apparently, that was who she wanted me to believe she was—just Liz.

*Wait a minute.* My brain was fuzzy.

"Wait, so you aren't Liz?" I asked, my mind back on track. Not the track I wanted it to be on, but she was the one who had thrown me the curveball.

"Jason, just—just—" She kept bouncing.

My eyes crossed, and my toes curled as she came down harder and harder on me. My fingertips dug into her hips as I held on for dear life. She was ferocious—and I loved it.

*Redheads.*

"It. Is. Fucking. Pru. Dence. Miss. Fucking. Pru. Dence. Say it," she cried out between broken breaths just as I started to spill out into her.

"Fucking Prude! Ence!" I shouted back at her as I pushed myself in deep, but even with my brain not working, I knew that didn't come out right.

Her cries softened into whimpers and then laughs as she collapsed headfirst into the space in front of her. I sat up, ready to apologize, but I was still flustered by whatever the fuck had just happened to my dick. I reached down to pat it and make sure it was still there and that she hadn't taken it with her on her wild ride.

"It's Dorothy. Elizabeth. Prudence. If you ever mutter it again, especially the way you just did, I *will* cut you up into those tiny stars we talked about.

Maybe keep you in a jar on my mantel. My forever jar of stars. Shakespearian-style." She laughed.

Thank goodness she laughed. *Phew.*

"I'm so sorry. I didn't know what was happening. Everything was just a tangle of moans and slippery wetness and searing heat, and your ass was bouncing me into oblivion. I meant for it to come out sexy. Believe me, you are no prude! Miss Liz ..." I rubbed my face into my hands, trying to wake some sense into my brain.

"Not for you, I'm not." She reached down and fondled herself, smiling up at me.

I was going to need a better sleep schedule, more energy, and a prescription to keep up with her.

*Redheads. Fuck, I love them.*

*Love? Shit!*

# 9

## LIZ

"Stay with me," he said.

My heart plummeted into my stomach as I thought about it. I hadn't slept with a man in years. Well, not sleep as in sex, but sleep as in really actually going to sleep beside a man—especially a man as sexy as Jason.

How would I ever calm down enough to fall asleep in his arms and drift off like they did in those romantic bedroom scenes in movies? I wondered if that ever really happened on the first night of being together anyway. I didn't think it had. There was just too much to worry about when you were sleeping with someone new.

I wondered if I would snore or maybe he would snore. Maybe I could sneak away in the morning before he woke up so that I could brush the morning breath out of my mouth before we did it—because I knew we would totally be doing it in the morning too.

*Also, do I wash my makeup off and possibly scare the shit out of him, or should I keep it on and dirty his pillowcase? What if I have a nightmare or talk in my sleep? What if I … sleep-fart?*

All of these thoughts ran through my head when he asked me to stay, but my heart wasn't on the same page—*typical*—because I muttered, "Yes," before I considered what all that entailed. "So, about this extra toothbrush …"

"I bought it just for you. It's pink and sparkly. It might be a kid's toothbrush, but I thought you'd like it anyway."

"It really is pink and sparkly? I need to see this extra-fancy toothbrush!"

"It is. Come look!"

I followed him into his brightly lit bathroom. It was so sterile and sparkling that I was sure he'd worked his ass off to make it this way for me. What kind of man would keep a bathroom like this for himself? None. They didn't make them this way. Men's bathrooms were only this clean if they wanted someone to see it—and preferably that someone would have boobs and be willing to put out. Me. It was me.

I leaned into the counter. My legs shook from the intense sex we'd had so many times that I lost count. That had never happened before, but I couldn't help myself. I was insatiable for Jason, and I thought he felt the same way about me. That look he had given me on the dance floor … that wasn't just pure lust but something more. Something like a longing, a wish. The same expression he had made that first night he told me about Kate.

I shivered as I realized Kate had lived here once, and tonight, I would be sleeping in her bed—with her husband. The same husband who had just screwed me senseless—or actually, I'd screwed him senseless a few of those rounds. I was on fire. It was that electricity we had. It filled me up just as he filled me up. I couldn't have asked for a better date night.

"This is the fanciest toothbrush I have ever seen! Even if it has a princess on it."

"Well, well, well, Princess Liz, I wouldn't give you anything less." He bowed down and cordially presented me the toothbrush like it was a crown of diamonds.

I would have gladly taken both the sparkly pink toothbrush and the crown of diamonds because he was right; I could be a bit of a princess—but an edgy one. And speaking of edge, edging Jason was on my sex bucket list next—right after being fucked up against the wall.

"Thank you." I bowed back at him.

"It's my honor, Your Majesty. I'll give you some privacy to get ready for bed. Need anything else? Want to sleep in a big T-shirt of mine? Or can you sleep naked next to me—please, please, please?"

"I'll take option two! And thank you, I'm good. Will just be out in a quick second."

I was grateful he'd left me alone as I took care of my business. The nurse in me told myself to go pee after sex, but I didn't want to ruin the moment—and I wasn't sure my legs would even work until they had a bit of a rest.

I turned on the faucet and brushed my teeth as I readied myself for sleeping with a damn-near stranger. Well, if I was being honest, Jason wasn't exactly a stranger. Not after what we had just done anyway. But still, it was nerve-racking, sleeping with anyone new.

*Cue my familiar anxiety.*

I glanced in the mirror. I definitely looked like I had been ridden hard and hung out to dry. I tried my best to clean myself up, but a hot mess I was, and hot mess was what he would be getting. I was exhausted after our marathon, and hopefully, he was too tired to notice my deterioration too.

I hobbled to bed, grateful for the dark. My eyes were heavy with sleep even though my heart still pounded in my chest. I tried to get comfortable but kept still so as not to bother Jason with all my tossing and turning. I was just too excited and anxious to go to sleep. Also, a little hungry again.

I replayed the night's events over and over in my head. I thought of the man who had sung that "Africa" song in the pizza place and the look on Tammy Tit-Knocker's face when Jason had said, "Bitch, I'm with Liz."

Okay, so he hadn't said *bitch*. I totally added that in there.

I thought about dancing at Whiskey Row and the way Jason's hands had felt me up in the dark and that look he'd given me that I was most surely overthinking—classic Liz.

I glanced at my jar of stars on the nightstand and smiled over how hard he'd worked to catch them for me—no doubt, he had known what he was doing. I was sure it had been a plan to get in my pants, and I was more than fine with that. Same with the charcuterie and the guitar. He'd obviously prepared, and he'd done a damn good job at it—all for me.

*Am I falling in love?* I mused. *I can't do that! I'm going to get hurt. I need to start pushing him away!* I panicked. *But what if this one time …*

I let my mind wander as I lay in bed and listened to the sounds of the whirring fan above us. Jason had rolled over, but I could tell by his breathing that he wasn't asleep yet. So far, this falling-asleep-in-each-other's-arms thing wasn't working. I was way over here, and he was way over there. I was confused but relieved. I was not responsible for the ninja kicks that my legs sometimes made in the middle of the night.

I felt my heartbeat still pounding through my veins as I closed my eyes and finally tried to drift off to sleep, my mind a blank slate. Peace, quiet, dark, silence—all things I needed to be able to actually fall asleep, but as soon as I had all of those things was when I heard him. The soft snores that came from the other side of the bed made me smile. I put my hand over my mouth to stifle my giggles, but my movement must have awakened him, as he stopped. I was aware that he was awake and probably lying there, wondering if I was too.

*Am I breathing too loud? Do I snore like that too? Is he lying there, knowing he just woke himself up with a big snarf and trying to play it cool? This is uncomfortable.*

My damn mind started to overthink again. Just when I'd thought I was about to drift off into la-la land with Mr. Jones, he'd had to open his mouth and sing—except this time, through his nose. I lay as still as could be, so he could get back to sleep. I didn't want him to know I was a bad sleeper. I would never be invited to sleep over again—which I had to admit, at this point, I would be okay with. I was tired as balls, and this just wasn't working for me.

I sighed to myself. The silence of the night was deafening. Now, it was too silent for me to sleep. See? I really was a hot mess—and that was an understatement. I burned hot and cold in every way imaginable.

I gazed into my jar of stars and tried to embrace the quiet, just as my stomach decided to rumble in protest for a midnight snack … or …

*No. Oh God, no.*

It wasn't a hungry rumbling. I knew that feeling. This was a rumbling that really was just not good—at all. This was a rumbling deep from within my bowels that echoed through the chambers of my shame. My heart raced as panic settled in. I needed to fart. Like, really bad. Really, really, really bad.

*Gosh damn it, Jason and your cheesy charcuterie!*

I blamed it on him even though I knew it had nothing to do with him. He just couldn't think perfect pink sparkles could blow her horn louder than he'd made me moan only moments ago. No, I couldn't have him thinking those kind of thoughts about me. He didn't need another Deuce in his life.

I tried to keep from whimpering as my body broke into a sweat. I felt the movement of air—aka a big fart—as it traveled through my intestines. If I looked down, I could probably see it too. A big lump floated around in there, like an alien about to burst forth in a colossal rip of stench. I held my breath and listened for Jason's breathing to see if he had fallen asleep yet.

*Nope, he's still awake. Fuck!*

I clenched my jaw and my butt and prayed to whoever would listen to me. *Please, please, please make this air inside me just magically disappear.*

And—*voilà!*—it did … after it groaned in frustration with the loudest *fuck you* inside my belly. A big, colon-rumbling, internal fart.

And then it did it again for an encore.

I held my breath to listen if he had fallen asleep yet.

*Nope.*

He suddenly got very quiet and very still. I knew he was holding his breath too. But not because he was weighing if I was asleep or not like I had been with him, but I guessed because he thought I'd farted in bed. And any fart that sounded like that put Deuce to shame.

*Oh my gosh, he thinks I farted. Kill me now. Should I say something? Should I tell him that totally wasn't a fart? Should I laugh it off? Should I just pretend and claim it? Is he going to say something? Is he going to laugh? Make a joke? Fuck, that's embarrassing! Should I just pretend I'm asleep?*

I settled with the latter choice and kept my mouth shut. I pretended I was dead-to-the-world asleep because I really wanted to be dead to the world. Here I was, in bed with quite possibly the sexiest man on the planet, and farting—correction, *internally* farting. And not just any internal farting. It wasn't like a cute, girlie, princess *poot*. Nope, it was a dinosaur *fart*. A fucking bronto-sore-ass, *claim it because that shit was impressive as fuck* fart.

He still held his breath. Maybe he would just hold it in his lungs until he died. Then, I wouldn't have to look him in the eyes ever again. Maybe it would all work out.

*Fuck it.*

I rolled onto my stomach, pushing into the mattress in hopes of quieting the journey my noxious gases had been making, but I wasn't sure my butt in the air was the right decision either. I closed my eyes and tried to bring my thoughts back to the sex. Yeah … the sex. Those blissful moments of hard-core fucking even if he had called me a prude. I smiled, thinking that if I'd been comfortable enough to tell him my real name, then I could surely handle an internal fart. And I was right because, moments later, Jason snored again, and I fell fast asleep. Internal fart forgotten. Well, not really. I would never forget that. I wondered if I should ever bring it up and clear the air, so to speak.

I woke to the smell of bacon and Deuce.

"Good morning, cutie. You're so cute. Yesh, you are! So ugly, you are cute. Mmhmm!" I babied him, scratching behind his half-ear while he excitedly squeaked out a fart. "Oh, wow. That will wake anyone up. Thanks, Deuce. I think I prefer the smell of bacon, but it's okay. I understand your gas struggles—trust me. Better out than in, right?"

My mind went to my own struggle the night before, and I quickly shook the thought back out. Today was a new day. I couldn't dwell on my bodily functions. I was a nurse, so it shouldn't have fazed me—even if it truly did and I knew it would until the day I died. Or at least, until our ten-year anniversary, and I could tell him, *Hey, honey, remember that time you thought I farted in bed on that first night?*

"Deuce! I'm sorry, Liz! He was supposed to be out there with me. I guess he pushed the door open. If he came to you instead of waiting on bacon, well, I'd say you have yourself a new best friend."

"He's fine. I liked being woken up by sweet snuggles."

"You do? Well then!" Jason jumped into the bed behind me and pulled me into him. "Come here, my little spoon!"

"I love being the little spoon!" I curled into his chest, his perfect biceps wrapping around me, holding me safe and secure.

"Good, because my spoon can't quit spooning you."

His cock thickened against my back, and I grew suddenly warm between my legs. It was so easy for Jason. Just the mutter of his name, and I was ready for action.

"But I made you something, and I can't go letting it get cold. Stay right here!"

He hopped back up and ran off. Deuce happily followed behind him. I sat up in bed and grabbed my jar of stars, making sure they were all okay. They'd been up late, partying too. I was excited to bring them back to my home and let them go. Maybe Jason would want to help me with that. Although, if Jason were to come do this little slumber party at my house, I would need to do a lot of prep. He'd obviously thought of it all, and, well, I just wasn't that much of a planner. I needed Team Jizz to come in and help woo him even though I knew, with one flash of my ass, he would already be wooed into that look ... that same one he had given me on the dance floor—the not-just-lust look, but not-quite-love look. *The falling look.* The same one I'd had plastered on my face for two days now.

"All right, Miss Fancy Pants! Tell me how you like this." Jason carried a tray full of food over to me in bed.

"Well, there's coffee, so you've already won me over, but what is this? This is beautiful!" I picked up and twirled a delicate flower that had been lying over my omelet.

"Nasturtium. Try it. It's edible. It has a peppery taste. There's a few inside the omelet too. It's a locally farmed pork sausage omelet with caramelized onions, nasturtium, goat cheese, and topped with a smoked tomato jam—all local ingredients, bacon included. The coffee is from a local roaster. I'm testing a few of them out for the shop too. I want to focus on local ingredients as much as I can."

I took a bite of the omelet and groaned. I was impressed, beyond impressed. As if last night hadn't been impressive enough, now, he threw this at me. Could he be any more perfect?

"Holy balls. This has to be on the menu! It has to. Why didn't you tell me you knew how to cook like this?"

"I didn't really know I could. I've just been toying around with things for the shop, and I've even impressed myself with that one."

"Come share it with me! Sit, eat."

"I already did. This is for you. It's not every morning I get to wake up to a beautiful lady in my bed. She deserves breakfast in bed every morning."

He moved down to the bottom of the bed and grabbed my feet, massaging them while he watched me enjoy his treats.

*Is this real life?*

"Thank you. For everything. Yesterday was amazing. This morning is amazing. All of it. I'd say you made up for the disastrous date nights a million times over."

"So, you're saying you would go on another date if I asked?"

*I'd do a damn lifetime if you asked.*

"I'd love to. Actually, I was wondering if you wanted to do next Saturday at my place. I can make you dinner. We can have a quiet night in. Netflix and chill." I grinned. "You can even bring Deuce, so he doesn't get too lonely."

"Aw, really? You'd let this stink muffin come along too? Well, aren't you just the sweetest thing!"

"I can be. Especially after you feed me bacon and tell me I'm pretty."

"Next Saturday it is then. In the meantime, I'll be working a lot in the café this week. If you ever get some free time, you are more than welcome to come on by and visit. I'd love that."

He kept massaging my feet as he smiled up at me. I noticed he had that look again. The falling one. He was falling, and I was too. It was happening, and I gladly resigned myself to it—even against my better judgment. If he could look at me like that, even after a night of internal farts, surely, Kate was out of the picture.

*Isn't she? Is that door finally closed? And if not, how can I slam it shut?*

I texted Jess.

> *Me: I wasn't careful. I tore my walls down. I'm doomed.*
>
> *Jess: But you crossed your heart and promised.*
>
> *Me: My heart and my head aren't on the same page, let alone in the same book. Remember? You know that.*
>
> *Jess: I know they aren't, and I knew you would fall. I already stocked up on booze and ice cream. Wanna talk about it?*

I immediately rang her phone. Of course I wanted to talk about it. I wanted to gush over everything and relive every moment. I wanted to sing from the mountaintops and sail across the ocean to let everyone know that Jason Jones was my lover and that I was falling in love. I hadn't fallen in love in a very, very long time.

"So, you're falling in love. You do know, he is still married, right?" Jess said.

"Why do you have to go and ruin it?"

"Ruin what? Did he say he wanted you and just you and that he was filing for divorce from a ghosting wife?"

"Well, not like that, but—"

"Okay, well, I'm not ruining it for you. I'm just trying to get your Jason-colored glasses off. You're seeing everything in rosy pink because he makes you feel good. And also because he's hot as fuck. But he has baggage."

"Are you going to listen to my night, or are we going to have a throwdown? Because I know he has baggage. You don't have to keep reminding me. I got it. It's tucked back into the tiny corner of my mind, and I'm ignoring it. I have to. It's too late for me, and I'm in this now, so it is what it is. Hopefully, his baggage is tucked away too."

I heard her let out a long sigh on the other end of the line, and I echoed it right back.

"I'm fucked, aren't I? I'm committing when I shouldn't be … again."

"Yes, no, maybe. I think you need to have the talk with him now before it goes any further. Ask him what his plans for divorce are and why exactly he hasn't filed yet. It's been years. If Kate is tucked into the back corner of his mind, why hasn't he just thrown her out and moved on? Why let her take up space? You need to be in that space. All of the space. You are amazing. You are worth it. You are first, always. You don't come second. Don't you dare let yourself go down that path—ever. I mean it. You're not a side bitch."

"I love you, Jess. Wish I could marry you."

"I feel like we've had this conversation before."

"About a dozen times."

"Will you learn?"

"Probably not."

"At least you're honest with yourself. But this time, you first. I won't make you promise not to go down this damn rabbit hole you keep going down. But you are such a strong and confident woman. Don't be a consolation prize. Be the grand prize, or don't even let him play to win."

"Working on that. Will you listen to my juicy details now that you've got that out of your system?"

"Wouldn't be doing my job as your BFF if I didn't get it out, but yes, lay it on me. Did Mr. Jones's tongue vibrate again?"

I recounted the whole night back to her, including the musical ensemble we performed at night. The snores and farts, not the moans and groans, although I recounted that to her too. I worked myself up so much as I relived the details that I would need a cold shower—or a hot one … with my vibrator. Just one thought of Jason's tight body slamming up against mine, and I was revved and ready to go. Electric tingles and all.

"So, he's coming over to your place this Saturday then?" Jess asked.

"Yes! So, I need your help. I'm going to start cleaning today and getting it super sparkly, but I need your help with some other stuff. Menu, drinks, et cetera, et cetera. I need to wow him like he wowed me."

"You're trying to be wifey material."

"Yes."

"You don't have to try, Liz. You are wifey material, but yes, I'll help. That's what friends are for—to plot shenanigans even if those shenanigans are making Jason fall in love with you and give you a happily ever after."

"You said it, not me."

"You're thinking it."

"I am what I am."

"The talk—have it before Saturday, okay? Make sure y'all are on the same page before you put in all this work and it blows up in your face. The only blowing up in your face you need is his cock blasting you. Maybe it will blast some sense into you. Keep it just sex until the talk."

"Okay, okay. Sheesh. I'll talk to him this week. He told me to stop by his shop anytime. Maybe I'll do it then."

"Love you. I'm here when you need me. Just let me know."

"Love you too, Jess. Thank you for being the bestest."

"Don't I know it."

I heard the defeat in her voice before she hung up. That made two of us.

I busied myself around the house, cleaning baseboards and ceiling fans. My house stayed pretty clean. No men, no kids, no pets. Plus, with my twelve-hour shifts at the hospital, I wasn't around much to mess it up. Nevertheless, I still found crevices that needed to be scrubbed, and I also decided to take my extra time to spruce up my back patio. I didn't have a fancy firepit like Mr. Jones or even a grill, but I did have a pool—and a pool boy.

Unfortunately, he was just a nerdy neighborhood kid and not some exotic, muscled-up sex fiend. But at least my pool stayed clean even if I never had a chance to get in it. For years, Jess and I had lain out there, working on our tans and day-drinking. We'd always ended up toasted—both drunk and sunburned. But we were much younger back then and much less busy. Now, she had a husband, and I … I had a jar of stars.

I picked up my jar just as Jason texted.

*Jason: Just letting you know, I really enjoyed last night. I'm outside on the patio, writing some music and thinking of you.*

*Me: I was just thinking of you too. I'm about to walk out back and release my jar of stars. Will send pic.*

I headed outside. I wished I could see stars at my place like I had at Jason's. But the city lights shone too bright. I hadn't even known what I was missing until last night. The night sky … the dreamy man. Living the life. That was what it was. I had built up my walls, too afraid to let myself go and commit, and now, I had learned I was missing living *the life*.

I opened the jar and set it on a table. The lightning bugs flashed off and on before they slowly made their way out, one by one. I sat and watched them, snapping pictures here and there. None of them turned out right, but I sent it over to Jason anyway. At least he could see a few flecks of gold and know that his stars were now mine.

*Jason: They made it! Now, you have some country stars in that flashy city of yours.*

I watched the fireflies glow until they all flew away, and once again, my backyard was dark. My night sky boring.

*You are my country star,* I started to type and quickly deleted it.

Jess was right; I had to have this talk before I let myself get any more deep in the feels.

> *Me: Your stars fit into my sky perfectly! They all flew up, up, up and away! I'm going to get in bed and get some sleep. I have an early shift in the morning. Good night, Jason. :)*

> *Jason: Good night, my little star.*

I paused before I set my phone down. I felt butterflies—or fireflies—as soon as I read his message. *His little star.* I melted into my seat. At least we were on the same page, I thought. Weren't we?

*If I am his little star, what does that make Kate? A black hole? A void still left in his soul? Can he just leave her out in space and take me to the moon?*

The butterflies—fireflies—swirled in my chest. This serious and uncomfortable talk I had to have with Jason was going to have to come quick.

# 10

## JASON

After last weekend, I thought of Liz all day, every day. One whiff of the peach trees that grew in my yard, and my mind was right back between her thighs. I was barely able to function at work, but my music suddenly took off. All of those lyrics that I'd told myself I would write down, I finally finished and then some. My songwriting skills improved tenfold, thanks to Liz—my muse.

I smiled at work, even when Brad was around, and much to everyone's notice. He even commented about how happy I seemed. Actually, it was more of a sneer than a comment. He *sneered* at my good mood. He also asked a lot of other questions, which was unlike him. He asked personal questions, financial questions, probing questions. I didn't know what he was getting at, and I was too distracted to figure it out.

Between Liz in my brain twenty-four/seven, my work in my own coffee shop, my late-night gigs, and dealing with Brad's bullshit schedule, I didn't have time for anything else. I clocked out every morning and went straight to my shop, meticulously checking off items on the list that Liz had tacked to the wall.

We texted back and forth all week, and she told me she would try to swing by today for a quick second during her lunch hour. I offered to get her lunch—no hot chicken this time—but she said she was on a time crunch. This week had been hectic at the hospital with back-to-school crap—whatever that meant. I imagined sick kids and dumbass teenagers injuring themselves, trying to be *cool*, but I wasn't a medical person and truly had no idea what she was talking about. I just knew that I really wanted to see her, and I'd been waiting for what felt like an eternity to have her lips back on mine.

"Knock, knock!" Liz stuck her head in the door.

"Hey you! You can just walk right in, you know. It's not like I'm spanking my monkey in here or anything."

"Well, that escalated quickly. I thought you much preferred choking your hot chicken. But I guess you do like spankings too."

I clutched her to me, closed my eyes, and breathed her in. *Peaches and cream.* The scent of her sent those electric tingles through my bloodstream again. I could feel, little by little, every part of me awakening—my cock specifically but also my soul. I was getting the warm fuzzies, an emotion I'd forgotten. If I was being honest with myself, I had never even felt this type of warm fuzzies—not even with my wife. This was different.

Whatever Liz and I had, I couldn't even begin to describe. I'd sing about it one day, I was sure. But I couldn't yet put it into words. It was just feelings—all the feels.

"Mmm, I'm happy to see you too," she said, breathless and panting. Her hands fumbled to my pants as she quickly unzipped them and pulled out my cock.

"I don't have a—"

"Shh! It's for you." She shushed me as I watched her lower herself to her knees.

I leaned against the counter to steady myself for what I knew was about to be another wild ride. She worked my hard length with her hands, grinning up at me before she licked the tip of my cock. My hands reached out to tangle in those gorgeous red waves of her hair. I gathered it in my palms and gently tugged as she bobbed her head up and down on my dick.

My head fell back, and I closed my eyes as I slid in and out of her warm, wet mouth. I was lost in the moment, growling and breathless when I heard her start to moan louder, breaking me from my trance. I glanced down and noticed she had her hand between her thighs, playing with herself … while she was playing with me.

*That is the sexiest damn thing.*

I felt my tension rising as I watched her. Her eyes locked with mine, and she smiled up at me, mouth full of my cock. I gripped her hair harder, pushing her into me. She flicked her hand between her legs faster and faster, matching my rhythm until I felt my searing hot cum shoot through me and spill out into her hungry mouth. She rolled her hips, trembling, as she swallowed me whole.

*Holy wow, that was fucking hot.*

She smacked her lips, licking me clean and giving me a look of satisfaction. I tried to give her a look of satisfaction back, but all I could do was grunt like a caveman. She had literally stupefied me.

"Now, show me this list you've been working on." She stood up, waiting.

"What? What list?"

"Your list I tacked up against that wall over there! You said you marked some things off." She giggled. She knew she had me wrapped around her finger after that little stunt.

"Oh, right, the list. Sorry, I just … my brain stopped working after you just came in here like a wild woman and gave me the best damn blow job ever."

"Really? The best? You must not have had very many then?" She cocked her head to the side and looked at me.

*Danger. Danger.*

"So, this list over here, yeah?" I changed the subject. *Crisis averted,* I thought.

I showed her the list and all I'd been working on. She walked around the place, impressed at how much cleaner and more put together it was. The coffee shop was finally beginning to look like an actual coffee shop.

"It's really coming together. I'm so excited for you! I wanted to tell you, I have a bit of time off next week, and I can help with whatever. Maybe we can tag-team this place and get it closer to being ready. I'll do whatever I can to help you get it off the ground. I believe in it, especially after that flower omelet.

You're going places, Jason Jones! You and your fancy-schmancy breakfast foods."

"Fancy, eh? You think? I thought you'd like that omelet. I'll have to let you be the official menu-tester. You can test the veggies since those are nasty! You can be honest with me. I don't think you'd blow smoke up my ass."

"I wouldn't. Which brings me to another conversation I wanted to have with you."

She moved closer to me and grabbed my hand. My body stiffened with her electric touch, except this didn't feel like a good *electric*.

*Danger. Danger.*

"I don't like the sound of this. Can't we just go back to the blow job? It really was the best I'd ever had. I—"

"Jason Jones!"

*Uh-oh.* She'd used my whole name. I was headed for trouble.

"Yes?"

"I'm being serious!"

"I know you are! That's why I'm getting scared over here. Look at me; my palms are sweating!" I stuck out my hands, palms up, and then rubbed them on my pants, fretting.

"Oh Lawd! You men. Nobody is dying. It's just that—"

"Did I snore the other night? It's that, isn't it? I'm so sorry. Look, I wanted to tell you beforehand, but I didn't know if ..." My voice trailed off as I caught the agitated look in her eye.

"Are you going to listen, or do you want to do the talking?"

She put her hands on her hips. Now, I really was in trouble.

"I apologize. I tend to ramble when I'm anxious. I'm all ears. This is serious Jason face." I looked at her as serious as I could, but I was pretty sure she could see the fear in my eyes.

"Serious Jason face. Right … what are we doing? I like you—a lot—but you're still married. Why? I'm having a hard time giving myself to you fully, if that's what you want, while you're still married. And yeah, yeah, I get it; she ghosted you, and you waited. But it's been years, and I'm worried you haven't moved on. I don't want to be a rebound or a backup plan. I'm slowly breaking my walls down for you and ready to give this a real shot. I just don't want to get hurt."

I bit my lip and stared at the ground. I couldn't meet her eyes.

"The truth is, Liz, I've not thought about Kate at all since I've been with you. I used to think about what she was doing or where she was or who she was with day and night. Every damn day and night. I always wondered. But then you showed up, and I got so lost in the fiery-red whirlwind that is you that I just haven't thought about my marriage—until recently. I wanted to talk to you about it too. I'm going to file for divorce and see how it all works without having someone there to sign papers. I put it off because I wasn't ready, but you … you make me ready. For anything. Even though I was married—and maybe this will sound terrible—I have never felt such strong feelings toward someone, wife included, until I met you."

"For real?"

"For real."

"So, what then? What is your plan?"

"I'll file this week. We can celebrate at your place, Saturday. I'll bring the champagne, and we'll toast to … new beginnings … together … if you'll have me."

"I'll have you any way I can get you, except married. So, I like this plan. We'll celebrate you working on getting that chapter closed, and we can celebrate opening up a new one. But, Jason, I don't want you doing this for me. I want you doing it for you. I don't want to pressure you into anything. If you don't feel ready to close that part of your life, then don't. It's why I wanted to talk to you, before things got too deep and our emotions were both too involved."

"I'm already deep, my little star, and I'm already involved. It's a done deal. I'll show you on Saturday." I leaned in and kissed her forehead, secretly praying that I really was done with the Kate chapter of my life. *Aren't I?*

A Divorce by Publication. That was what I had to file for, according to my lawyer. I had to basically shout it from the rooftops that I, Jason Jones, wanted to divorce my ghosting-ass wife. I had to show intent that I'd thoroughly searched for her by submitting an affidavit—easy enough. I'd have to appear before a judge and put my wishes for divorce in the newspaper for a few weeks.

On one hand, I was glad that I had kept all of my research into her disappearance, as this would hopefully go more quickly and easily than I imagined. On the other hand, it was still totally a pain in the ass, and I hated airing my business in public. But then again, who actually read the paper anymore anyway?

I spent two days running around town to get my divorce shit in order so that I could present it to Liz on Saturday like a trophy, for a trophy. She was my trophy, my little star, my fiery phoenix, my fantasy and desire, my Liz. I had it bad. It must have been the blow job. That would do it every time. I was ninety-nine percent sure she knew that too. She'd used the whole *buttering me up before she broke the news* scenario, and like any other red-blooded man, I hadn't cared. I liked to be buttered up—with Liz's sloppy blow jobs especially.

I filled out the paperwork in the office to get it done and over with before I had time to think about what I was doing. Letting go was hard for me, obviously. But now, knowing Liz, it wasn't as bad as I'd thought it would be. She had helped me so much. I was pretty sure this was the right thing to do. I felt it in my soul. Life was finally looking up for me.

I happily made my way back to the coffee shop and ticked another item off of my list—inspections. That had been earlier today, and I felt pretty damn good about it. Almost everything was in working order, even the water that I had quickly turned on right after the hot-chicken fiasco. The only things I had left, besides buying furniture and cleaning, would be hiring and booking. I already planned to be part of the opening gig so that I could thank all of the locals who supported me.

Liz had told me she would help with the furniture and decor next week. Things were rolling along smoothly—almost too smoothly. I had a bit of anxiety that life was too good to be true. Something bad was bound to happen. That was how it always worked. The universe couldn't be perfect, if even for a moment—in my experience. I tucked that bit of negativity in the back of my mind and continued working. I crossed my fingers that my next and last inspection would go well. My funds were running out, and I was starting to panic.

*Me: Got champagne and paperwork for tomorrow. Anything else I need to bring?*

*Liz: Yay!!! So glad you got it done. You can bring some swimming trunks! We can go for a late-night dip in my pool.*

*Me: You have a pool? Do I really need swimming trunks? ;)*

*Liz: Yes, and good point. Although I think I might even like seeing you in a banana hammock. That might be hot.*

*Me: I don't even own one of those, but for you, I'll wear anything.*

*Liz: Now, we're talking. I've got a few more things to pick up for Saturday, but I'll be here, ready at five. Does that sound okay?*

*Me: It sounds perfect. See you at five tomorrow.*

I set my phone down and did a happy dance. *Champagne and pool sex? Cha-fucking-ching. Bring it on, Saturday!*

I had only one day left to get my shit together. Meaning I needed to find a new outfit, preferably off a mannequin. I also had to work at my real job, wash my truck, play another gig, and get my hair trimmed. Not cut, just trimmed. Liz loved to run her hands through it, and I loved it when she did that too. I also had to hunt down a banana hammock and pick up another bouquet, but this time, it needed to say something *more* … something like *I'm ready to be yours, and I want to make you mine.*

I was still dancing around the back of my shop when I heard the door open. The inspection guy had already been here; surely, he hadn't forgotten something. I peeked around the corner to see who would dare disrupt my joyous shenanigans, and there he stood, tall, dark, and ugly—Brad. My jaw dropped as soon as I saw his squished-in, angry face, like a peeled apple that had been left out to rot in the sun. I realized that not only was I an employee of his, but I was also his competition … and now, he was aware of that.

*Fuck you, universe,* I thought.

I had done my happy dance too soon. I had known something would kill my mood. That little ball of dread that popped up when my life had been going fantastic always proved to be correct. In Jason Jones's world, life couldn't ever be good for long.

"Well, well, well. Looks like you have quite the setup here." He shuffled inside, taking my pride and joy all in with his beady little eyes.

"Thanks. I've been working hard on it."

"So I see. So I see." He slowly walked around the kitchen area, reaching out and touching the espresso machines—*my* espresso machines.

"Can I help you with anything?"

"I don't think so. I just know you've been so busy lately with all the time you've requested off and all."

"You mean, the two hours I requested to leave early yesterday? You think I'm busy because, in my entirety of working for you, I've requested maybe half a day off? Total? That tipped you off?"

"Yes," he sneered.

"You know employees do have personal lives … *people* have personal lives. I didn't think I was obligated to tell you what I did in my free time. Is that some type of law or something?" I played dumb, but I was also getting really, really pissed off that he had the audacity to come in here with his smug mug.

"No, not at all. I was just curious when I heard a new coffee shop was opening, and then, well, when I heard who was behind it, I was a bit shocked that you hadn't told me. I'm guessing it's because you were stealing my secrets to my successful business, so you could run them over here."

I clutched my sides and laughed. *What a fucker.*

"My coffee shop will be nothing like yours. The only thing we will have in common is coffee. So, yes, actually, thank you for hiring me to learn how to make coffee. Even though someone else had taught me, thanks for hiring me."

"Great! Glad I could help, and since I've given you all the knowledge you need, you're fired!"

"Fired! For what? For scaring the pants off of you with your latest competition?" I asked as the coward rushed out.

"We'll see just how well you can really do, Jason Jones. You're just a second-rate singer, and you make shit coffee. Your check will be in the mail. Don't come back to my store." He slammed the door shut.

*Second-rate singer? Shit coffee? No job? Fuck.*

I was screwed. With money tight and my small business loan running out, I needed to work even if it was a piddly shit job like the one I'd had with Brad. I went to the back of the shop, the only place with a makeshift chair and desk, and I put my head in my hands to close my eyes and concentrate on what the fuck would happen next. I could pick up some extra gigs, apply for another business loan, and …

*Be a male stripper?*

No, I couldn't work nights doing that *and* perform gigs.

I resigned myself to reaching out to a few booking agencies I'd worked with in the past. Perhaps they would have even more gigs for me. I stood back up and began to make a list of contacts and to-dos. This list thing Liz had taught me had been coming in handy lately. I was halfway through my contacts when I heard the door open again. I was sure Brad was back for me. He lived on drama.

"Fuck you, Brad! I'm not a second-rate singer, and I don't make shit coffee! You just buy shitty coffee! And another thing, asshole, you—" I called as I made my way back toward the entryway.

"Jason?"

I recognized her voice before I even saw her. The familiar and sweet way she had always said my name in two long-drawn-out syllables—*Jay-son.* My knees felt weak as I put one foot in front of the other and stepped out of the hallway and into her view.

"Kate," I breathed her name out as if I let out a four-year-long sigh of relief.

She looked the same as the morning she'd left, when I kissed her good-bye and headed into work, only to come home to her already gone. The only thing that was different about her was the unease in her eyes.

"I'm sorry," she said, slowly inching closer to me, her eyes darting toward the corners of the room, never at me.

"Are you okay? You don't look so good. I'll save the *where the fuck have you been* until you tell me that you are all right." I stepped closer toward her, afraid she would fall. "Seriously, you look like you're about to pass out. Back from the grave, I take it?"

"I'm so sorry. I just … I thought …"

The words caught in her throat as she fell into my arms.

*Fuck you, universe.*

I laid Kate down in my truck just as she was coming to. Her frail body stirred, slumped in the seat next to me. I was about to take her to the hospital because what the fuck else was I supposed to do? I'd honestly assumed at this point that she was dead because how could anyone—*anyone*—especially a spouse, up and disappear on someone they loved like that?

"Jason!" She sat up, startled and obviously confused as to where she was.

"I'm taking you to the hospital, but are you going to tell me what's going on? Where have you been? Why did you leave like that? I'm trying to keep my temper in check now that I know you aren't dead, but I want answers. Spill it."

"No, no hospitals. Please. I'm fine. I really am. I'm just … going through a lot. Can we go home?"

I saw the color returning to her face and knew then that she really was fine. She had a lot of explaining to do.

"Home? Where are you living?"

"At our house?" she whispered, still not meeting my eyes.

"Um, no. You don't have a place to go?"

"No."

"Fuck!"

"I'm sorry."

"Sorry doesn't cut out four years of ghosting someone. You made vows to me!"

"I know. I'll explain. I promise. I think I just need to lie down a bit."

She rested her head against the window of my truck. The asshole in me wanted to tell her to go away, but I wasn't an asshole. And if I was, it was only by a smidgen. I even had to try hard at that. I was a certified sweetie pie, and everyone knew it, even me. I opened doors *and* held hands. I paid the ticket *and* pulled out chairs. No shame here. I liked that chivalrous shit. It made me feel good, and it made panties come off faster.

"We can go back to *my* place. But only for you to rest tonight. I have plans this weekend *and* a life I need to get back to. You know, the life you walked out on."

"I'm so sorry. So sorry."

She closed her eyes as I started my truck and headed home. The silence settled in on us comfortably. It was much more comfortable than if we had been discussing just what the hell was happening. I knew I hadn't hit rock bottom yet because I still needed to tell Liz.

*Fuck you, universe! Seriously! Fuck you!*

# 11

## LIZ

I woke up bright and early Saturday so that I could head to the farmers market for some local snacks that Jason and I could try. I was so excited for his coffee shop and impressed that he was doing what he could to give back to the community. He was such a sweetheart. I'd told my sisterhood at work all about him and his soon-to-be opening café, and they had all agreed that they would spread the word. He would have a lot of customers from the hospital at least.

The last time I'd been in his shop, it had really looked like it was coming together. Pretty soon, he and I would be sitting, hand in hand, sipping lattes and munching on bacon—locally sourced, of course. I couldn't freaking wait!

I put my hair up in a ponytail and skipped out the door just as my phone vibrated in my purse.

*Who the heck is calling me this early?*

I fished my phone out and saw Jason's name flashing across my screen.

"Hey! I see you're up early. Making those fancy omelets again? I was just on my way to track down that bacon jam and some other goodies for tonight."

"Liz—"

"Anything I can pick up for you?"

"Liz, I can't come tonight."

My heart plummeted into my stomach.

"Oh."

"Look, Kate showed up yesterday. Also, I got fired, but that's another story for another time. My main issue right now is Kate."

"What?" I sat down on my doorstep as my world started to spin. "Your wife, Kate?"

"Yes. She's back, and I-I let her stay here last night. Just for the night because she didn't look too good. Like something was wrong with her. We talked and got things sorted, I think. But I've got to help her get on her feet. She has no place to go. I'm sorry, Liz. Can we reschedule it?"

*Such a sweetheart, such a fucking sweetheart,* I thought as I chastised myself for believing I was okay to finally let my walls down.

I felt the tears building up in my eyes as I took a deep breath, hoping that he wouldn't hear the crack in my voice when I spoke, "Okay."

"I feel like such a shithead. I don't know what to do, Liz. She obviously needs my help, and I don't want to let you down. I want to be with you. I was looking forward to tonight, to you. I needed that. But what was I supposed to do?"

*Tell her she lost her chance when she disappeared and wrecked your life.*

"I don't know," I lied. I wanted to ask why she'd left and what they talked about, but it wasn't any of my business, and I didn't trust my voice on hiding my emotions any longer. I needed to get off the phone—ASAP.

"Hey, I know we were supposed to go shopping next week for the shop. Can we still do that? We can talk then. I'll tell you everything. I know you've got questions. Maybe … hopefully … by next week, she will be gone."

"Sure. Next week."

"Thanks! I'll keep in touch. Maybe I can get rid of this problem sooner rather than later."

"Okay."

"Bye, Liz."

"Bye, Jason."

I picked myself up off of my doorstep and headed back inside. The sun had been shining down on me, but all I wanted was dark. I needed to be in the dark—alone. I dropped my purse to the floor, took my hair down, and stripped my clothes off as I crawled back into bed.

*Now that his wife is back in the picture, where does that leave me? Fuck my life. When the going gets good, the good gets going. Or something like that … I think.*

And to think, I had slowly been breaking my walls for that turd nugget.

*Classic Liz, one mistake after the other. I will never be someone's second choice—except he isn't exactly choosing her, is he?*

All he had told me was that she was back and he was helping her get on her feet. So, now what? I had so many questions.

*Why is she back? Why does he have to help her? Is she on drugs? Does she want to get back together with him? Does he want to get back together with her? Are they sleeping in the same bed? Does she still love him? Is she going to be okay? Can she please get her shit together and leave him the fuck alone? Can he get his closure now? Does he think I really farted in bed the other night?*

I was torn between being pissed off and being in tears, so I settled for both. I wasn't exactly sure why I was so mad. It wasn't like he had really done anything terrible. I mean, I guessed it was great and all that he wanted to help her when she was down, but what the fuck? She had ghosted him. She had broken his heart. She hadn't been there when he needed her. She had left, checked out, and vanished. She hadn't cared. If she had cared, she would have never treated him that way. I would never treat him that way. I had been prepared to give Jason the world if he asked, and I'd thought that he was starting to feel the same about me. But now? Now, I was sitting here, waiting on a man to give me some answers. I was doing exactly what I'd said I wouldn't do.

I dialed Jess's number.

"Jess?" I called through the phone.

"What are you doing up so early? Are you okay? What's wrong?"

"She's back."

"Who's back?"

"His wife—"

"Oh shit. When did she get back? Is she there with him? Now?"

"Yes, and supposedly, she came back yesterday. She's staying with him. He's going to try to help her get on her feet or something like that."

"What. The. Fuck? So, now what?"

"I don't know. He said he would let me know, and we can reschedule the date."

"Oh no, honey. Nope. You can't be sitting around, waiting on his phone call to tell you if he is back with his wife or not. No, ma'am. I'm getting my shit together right now. I'll be over there in five minutes."

"Jess, you don't have to. You warned me, and I didn't listen."

"Are you kidding me? This is some crap! I'm not going to let my BFF figure it out alone. Team Jizz is going to conquer this drama. You know how many times you helped me in the past with my ex-boyfriends and dumb mistakes? I still owe you probably four hundred times over! You'll not be sitting over there, alone in your anxiety. We're getting to the bottom of it."

"Okay. If you say so. You know where the spare key is. Love you, Jess."

Before I hung up the phone, I heard her screaming to her husband that she was having a Jizz emergency and would be back later. Jess would help. She was always there for me.

I pulled the sheets up over my head and sighed. That was what I deserved for getting involved with a married man. Except he wasn't really married—or at least, he wasn't until she had shown back up, I thought. This was too much drama and confusion, even for me.

I remembered that look in his eyes when he had talked about her. I remembered how his voice had almost caught in his throat when he spoke her name … and then … and then he had looked at me like that. That night on the dance floor, he'd had the same sparkle in his eyes. He'd even told Tammy Titty that I was his.

*Am I just a rebound for him?*

I was still in bed, wiping my snotty nose and tears, when I heard Jess barge through my front door.

"Liz?"

"In here!" I called from the bedroom.

"Geez Louise! I should have known. Get up!"

She stood at the doorway, her arms loaded with chips, ice cream, and booze.

"I don't want to get up. I want to lie down here and contemplate life." I rubbed the tears from my eyes.

"Let's contemplate it by the pool. We haven't done a day of swimming and day-drinking for a while. Look, I got stuff for mimosas!"

She took the champagne out of her bag and held it up, dangling it in front of me like it was a carrot on a stick and I was a dumb horse.

*Neigh, neigh.*

I groaned as I pulled myself up and out of my security blankets.

"Don't you think lying out in the sun and day-drinking will be another bad decision?" I asked.

"Nope."

"Whatever you say! Just give me the champagne!" I grabbed the bottle and slumped my shoulders.

*Champagne. He was supposed to bring me champagne.*

It was half past four when Jason texted.

*Jason: Do you have a minute to talk?*

"Jess!" I screamed excitedly like a schoolgirl.

I startled Jess into going overboard.

We'd been floating around the pool all day long, only stopping to get a refill on booze and junk food. We'd even called Luke to bring us over more greasy snacks. He'd been our makeshift pool boy for the day, even providing us with some much-needed laughs here and there. But most of all, he graciously hadn't mentioned Jason or the date we were supposed to have, so he could meet him. Luke was either super smart, or Jess had cracked the whip on him. I thought it was a little bit of both.

"What the fuck?" Jess came up out of the water and coughed. "You'd better be dying because you scared the hell out of me! Now, look! My hair's all wet, and I probably have raccoon eyes!" she slurred.

"He texted me!" I slurred back.

"What?"

"Jason! Jason texted me." *Hiccup.*

"Well? What's it say?" Jess rubbed her eyes, smearing mascara down her face like she was wearing war paint—which going to war was a good way of describing our day.

We'd spent the entire day reminiscing over all of our past mistakes. There was … a lot. We'd relived some good memories, like spring break 2011, and some not-so-good memories, like spring break 2011. That had been a rough year.

We'd done everything we could to forget about Jason after we decided together that it would be best to just forget. If Jason wanted me, he'd let me know.

He would come after me. I was supposed to be the strong, independent woman and not chase him. I'd crossed my heart—again—and promised Jess I would leave it be this time unless he contacted me first. Thankfully, he had because I very much wanted to chase him—or at least, drunkenly stumble to him.

"He wants to know if I can talk."

"Shit. Did you respond? Oh my gosh, Liz, did you drunk-text him?" Jess started to hiccup.

"No. Not yet."

"If you go down this path, Ayesha might come out, and you'll not be able to recover from that chick. She will give him an ass-whooping that will probably send him straight outta Nashvegas."

"But I'm not mad, just sad. I think"—*hiccup*—"that Ayesha is gonna be fine. She's gone away for now. It's just Liz. Lonely Liz." I felt the tears starting to well up in my eyes. This always happened if I drank too much.

It could go one of two ways. Okay, one of three ways. I could get sick, which happened plenty. I could turn into Ayesha again—wasn't proud of that either. Or I could turn into a big ball of tears and all *woe is me* as the world came crashing down onto loser Liz.

"Don't. Just ignore him. Respond tomorrow. When you're sober," Jess begged.

I was already holding the phone as close as I could to my eyeballs, squinting, and in deep concentration, I texted him back.

*Me: I am sad.*

*Jason: Okay ... me too. That's what I wanted to talk to you about. You busy?*

*Me: No justs sad.*

*Jason: Okay …*

*Me: Why this wek? Why aftre all I did? Why no?w*

*Jason: I'm sorry. I don't understand. Are you okay? I'd like to call you and have an actual conversation if you are available to talk on the phone.*

*Me: Fine. Give me 10 mineuts pls*

"Quick, Jess! Get water! I have to be sober to remember this! He's"—*hiccup*—"calling!"

Jess moved at a turtle's pace, though no doubt, in her mind, she was Speedy Gonzales. She, too, had indulged too much. I laughed as I watched her walk through the water like it weighed a ton. She looked as if gravity was pulling her in the opposite direction as she fought her way out of the pool, complaining all the way.

"You owe me. You so owe me." She stared into me with her drunken, narrow eyes.

"Don't I know it!" I laughed.

It was hard to stay sad when I had Jess around. Also when I had mimosas—lots of them. I quickly drifted back into Loser Liz Land as she went inside, and things became silent. Like my brain. I felt so empty.

I splashed the cool pool water on my face, tried to shake myself sober, grabbed my towel, and headed toward a chair—any chair. If I didn't sit down soon, I would wobble over at any minute—partly because of my always-lingering anxiety and partly because of my not-always-but-maybe-too-much-present drunken stupor.

*Deep breaths. Deep breaths.*

I counted to ten, twenty, forty before Jess came back with my water.

"You are so deep in the feels. Look at you! What the hell? Do you need a paper bag, so you don't hyperventilate? Does Jason have like a magic-wand dick or something? One flick and swish, and you're under his spell?" She held her hand out in front of her crotch, swishing and flicking an invisible wand and then shaking it at me.

"Pretty much."

"Figures. Luke too. That's how I knew I had a keeper, except Luke wasn't married."

"Burn." I flinched.

My phone started to vibrate in my hands.

*Here goes nothing.*

"What up?" I answered in a manly *this is cool* voice that surprised me just as much as I was sure it surprised him.

*Fuck, wrong approach.*

Jess's mouth hung open beside me. She was either about to hurl or laugh. Who knew? It could go either way at this point. We were Team Disaster. But a much-needed disaster. It'd been a long time since we gave no fucks and acted like idiots. Okay … it hadn't been that long, but it had been a long time since we had a pool day. There was a lot of lost time to make up for, and like any bad decision we had ever made, we were making up for it all in one day.

"Hey, Liz! You still sad? Is it because of what happened? Because I canceled tonight?" Jason said.

"It's because I cleaned my house top to bottom, bought new pool floats we could fuck on, got my hair done, waxed my biscuit, and planned on cooking a really fancy-schmancy meal tonight, but there's just one thing missing. Uh-oh. I'm alone." If I had a whip, I would have cracked it. I even felt the sting in my voice. Ayesha had entered the building.

"Pool floats we can fuck on? Those must be some sturdy pool floats because you know that I like it wild."

"I do too. Wild and unmarried." I dug my claws in deeper.

"Phew. Okay, let's just dive right in. See what I did there? Dive?"

I let the awkward silence on the phone remain. My nerves were rattled, but this was bullshit, and I wasn't going to *he-he-he* and fake giggle my way through it.

"So," he continued, "remember how I said I liked to think she was on some tropical island with an exotic man named Pedro?"

"Uh-huh," I answered.

"His name is Rico. Yep. Ironic, huh? Fucking Rico Suave. Just kidding. I don't know his last name. Anyway, Rico, who she conveniently met online, promised to whisk her off to his palace in Bosnia. Fucking Bosnia. I had to look that shit up on a map. I had no idea where it was!"

"Okay."

"So, she went to Bosnia and slummed it with Rico Suave, who, crazy enough, didn't own a palace in Bosnia. He owned a hut in Bosnia. Also, two llamas, but that's beside the point. That's all he had."

"Got it. So, why is she back?" I didn't give a fuck about Rico, Bosnia, or llamas. I only wanted to know if Kate was back to take my man—or was he still her man? My nostrils flared.

"She stayed and tried to make it work because she loved him, and she had a quiet life over there and blah, blah, blah. According to her, he left her though. Pulled the same shit on another chick he met online, and now, she said she's back to make things right."

"What exactly does *make things right* mean?"

"She said she only wanted to apologize, explain herself, and be on her merry way. She just had no place to go. She's looking for a job, and I'm going to help find her an apartment. I just—"

"You what?"

I was suddenly sober. Kind of.

"I told her I would help her find an apartment," he said slowly and very, very carefully.

"So, she's staying."

"In Nashville?"

"Yes."

"Yes. But not with me. I'm helping her with an apartment, like I said …"

"But she is with you, in your house now?"

"Well, yeah. She only just got back. I can't go and abandon her."

"She abandoned you."

"You're right. She did. But I'm not an asshole. I'm not one to walk out on someone like that."

"What are you doing to me?"

"Not walking out on you, if that's what you're hinting at. I called to tell you what is going on. Please give me this chance, Liz. I'm getting her out as soon as I can. I even told her about us."

"Yeah? What did she say?"

"That she's happy for me."

"I bet she is." I rolled my eyes. *Bullshit.*

"So, come by the shop on Monday, as planned. We can do the furniture and decor shopping, okay?"

"So, you called to tell me that your wife ran off with another man, she's back and you're taking care of her, but you want me—the person you're dating or your girlfriend or whatever the fuck I am to you—to help you with your shop still next week. While your wife is home. *Your wife.*"

"Basically. But damn, it doesn't sound good when you say it like that."

"How else should I say it?"

"That you, who I do actually consider my girlfriend, are helping me get rid of my wife."

"Where's the shovel?"

I heard him suck in his breath.

"I walked right into that one, didn't I? Redhead and all. Just say you'll stick by me while I do what I need to do to get us back on track and fucking on that pool float. Please? You're my little star. My nights haven't been shining without you. I don't want to be in this drama, but it is what it is. I'm thinking of it this way: I will have closure once it's all done. So, at least I got that going for me."

I relaxed into a puddle when he said I was his star again. A sopping wet, champagne, and melted ice-cream puddle. I looked over at Jess, who was dozing on the chair beside me. Thankfully, she wasn't watching me do all of this stupid melting. I crossed my heart after all. *Team Jizz!*

"Let's get you some furniture. But now that she's back, I guess you can go get the divorce papers instead and have her sign on Monday."

"I'm already a step ahead of ya. You'll see. Monday. Meet me at the shop around one? I think I'll be done by then."

"Deal. See you then."

"Bye, Liz."

I hung up the phone, unsure of how I felt. On one hand, I was smitten, and on the other hand, I was pissed. I wanted Jason, but I wanted him to myself.

I texted Luke to come get his snoring wife so that I could head into the shower and go to bed early. The sun and the drama had worn me out.

The next few days, I busied myself with projects around my home. I didn't want to clean my closets out, but I did. I didn't want to pull weeds out of my flowerbeds, but I did. I didn't want to organize my junk drawer because who really did that? But I did. I did anything and everything to keep my mind off of Jason and Kate. Anytime I felt my mind start to wonder about what they were really doing over there at his firepit, I would start to clean out another drawer or closet. By the time I was done on Monday morning, I had eight bags of clothes and goodies to donate to the homeless shelter. In one of those bags was my sparkly cowboy boots.

I loaded my car up to head to the shelter before I was to meet Jason at his shop. I hadn't heard from him yesterday or this morning, and I began to worry that he'd forgotten … or that he was too busy banging Kate to remember his *star*.

I turned the music up in my car and rolled the windows down. The weather was getting a little cooler, and the leaves were starting to turn. Autumn was my favorite time of the year. It was perfect firepit weather—with Jason. I thought his backyard would look amazing when the leaves all changed. I hoped to see it.

My phone dinged just as I pulled into the donations drop-off at the shelter. I wasn't the most popular person. If my phone dinged, it was either Jess, work, rarely my mom, and now Jason.

*Jason: I'm at the shop. Revved and ready!*

*Good*, I thought.

He could wait a little bit. I was running late and playing games. I didn't want to keep him waiting, but I did it anyway. How pathetic would I look if I was there on time and an eager beaver? I didn't want him to know he had been on my mind all this time. Then, he would have the upper hand, and that just wasn't going to fly with me. Even if he did have the upper hand because, like Jess had said, I had let myself stupidly fall deep into the feels. I had been falling ever since he spanked my ass and told me to call him Mr. Jones. It was that magic wand of his in his pants that had done it. I blamed it on that, not my desperation.

When I'd first met Jason, the only desperation I'd had was to get laid. It was just that he was so damn good at it and that he easily made me into mush. And then he wooed me with all of his efforts he put into our date nights, the jar of stars, the firepit, and Deuce.

I even missed Deuce, and I'd only seen him once. It had all been too perfect. That electrifying touch meant something. I knew it, and Jason knew it. Now, if only we could get Kate to realize it and run away again, I would be good. I wondered if he had felt tingles with Kate.

I drove around town, belting out girl-power songs to rev myself up for our rendezvous at the shop. By my timing, I would only be thirty minutes late. I would let him wait and let him wonder.

*A dose of his own medicine*, I thought as I finally parked my car and headed into his café.

"Hey there, gorgeous!" he said, embracing me as soon as I walked through the door.

"Sorry I'm late!" I gave no excuse, but at least I did apologize.

"That's okay. I got some odds and ends finished around here. And check it out." He held up a document—divorce papers.

"So, it's done then? She signed?"

"No, not exactly. The laws are dumb. It takes ninety days from the time we sign, if she doesn't fight me on anything. She hasn't signed yet, but I'm going to get her to do it tonight."

"So, she's still staying with you?"

"Only for a few more days. She's sleeping in the spare bedroom. I know you've been wondering that. I would too." He leaned in and kissed my forehead. "I'm not a married man, Liz. I mean, technically, I am, but she left a long time ago, and we are through. We are only married on paper, and after this"—he held up the papers—"this means it's a done deal, and she can be gone and out of my life for good!"

"How are you not angry with what she did? How are you okay with it all?"

"Not angry? Are you kidding me? I was seething mad when she told me what she did. I thought, at first, she was on drugs or something because she looked terrible! So, I didn't feel like I could be upset about that as much because she would need help. But, turns out, I was right, and she just wanted to live that Rico fucking Suave life in Bosnia, so yeah, I was pissed."

"But not pissed enough to kick her out."

"I have my limits. It is tense, cold, and icy at my house. The only talking we have done is short and not so sweet. I told her when she will move out, and I told her she will sign these papers—today. I think I have been fair, even letting her stay at all."

"You're a good man, Jason Jones."

I tried to smile but failed miserably at it. I was feeling bad about feeling bad. I should be happy he was treating this woman, his soon-to-be ex-wife, kindly. Even if she was a bitch for running off with another man, Jason still had the decency to support her in a time of need. I did see the honor in him doing the right thing like that, but I didn't have to like it. I certainly would not have been that nice. Ayesha would have come out as soon as she stepped through my door, if she had been my runaway spouse.

"I am pretty good, aren't I? So good that I'm going to take you shopping and let you make this place awesome. Let's go!"

He swept me off of my feet. Literally. He picked me up, and I wrapped my arms around his neck and laughed. I thought things were going to be all right now. He had the papers, and I had him.

"Are you sure you want to go shopping with me? I might have this place covered in glitter! You know how I'm so extra and all," I teased.

"Glitter? So it can shine like you? My star?"

"Jason Jones! You have such a way with words—and women!"

I smiled as he carried me in his arms and out the door.

# 12

## JASON

How the hell I'd ended up with two women in my life, I didn't know. But here I was, with my girlfriend, Liz, and my soon-to-be ex-wife, Kate, who still hadn't signed the papers. It was going on day five now after I'd asked her to, and still, she was giving every excuse in the book. She said she wasn't feeling well, she was getting her paperwork together, she had to find her own lawyer, she was busy looking for a job, and the list went on and on and on.

But, today, Liz called, and she wasn't happy.

Things had been tense all week long as we worked together in the shop. I could tell she wanted to know more about why Kate was there and when she would be leaving. I'd offered up all the information I could, but the problem was, I didn't have a lot of information myself. Yes, I wanted Kate to leave too. And Kate knew that she only had by the end of the weekend to get into an apartment. But she was still there, and Liz was still here—though I sensed Liz wouldn't be here for much longer if I couldn't get rid of Kate.

With each new day that nothing had changed in my marital status, Liz grew more and more distant. I didn't blame her. Our relationship couldn't move forward with a third party involved, so what was the point? I didn't expect her to wait on me or Kate, no matter how much I hoped she would.

"Hey, look!" I said as I showed her that our to-do list was almost finished.

The furniture had arrived before the weekend, and we'd spent the entire day unboxing it all and setting it up.

"Oh, yeah! Now, all you have to do is hire and train some employees, right? Do you have anyone in mind?"

"Well, it's not like I can step foot back into Brad's place, but I'm pretty sure I know two or three workers there who would come over here and work with me in a heartbeat. I don't have their contact info, so I'll have to sneak over there at some point, but it's a start."

"Have you thought about hiring Kate? I know you mentioned she is looking for a job."

"Hell no!" I cut her off, much to her satisfaction.

I knew she was curious about my feelings, and despite my numerous attempts at telling her how I felt about the whole situation, she still was skeptical. She had hinted around to her commitment issues well enough that I knew I had to take extra care with her, and so far, I was doing a shit job at it despite my efforts.

"I don't want Kate here. I don't even want her at my house!" I said.

"She won't be after this weekend, right?"

I heard the hope in her voice, and I was sure she could hear the nervousness in mine.

"That's what I told her. She said she had an interview yesterday. I didn't ask her how it went. I told her, tomorrow, I'll take her looking for a place, and she can—"

The door to the shop opened, and speak of the devil herself, Kate walked right in.

*Oh shit.*

"Kate! Hi!" I said. My voice was about ten decibels too high, like I'd been kicked in the nuts, which was a very fitting analogy for this fucked up predicament I found myself in.

"Oh. I'm sorry. I didn't know you had company. I'll just—" She turned to go.

"Kate. I'm Liz. It's nice to meet you." Liz stood up and walked the short distance to the door to greet Kate, and I was pretty sure it was also to mark her territory. "Come sit down. We were just discussing you actually."

*Uh-oh.* I tightened my jaw, my fists, and even my asshole. This wasn't going to be good.

"Oh, really? Great. Well, since I'm here, in the middle of your Kate meeting, do tell me what it was you were discussing. My super-shitty decision-making skills? My many stupid mistakes? My broke-ass circumstances? My fucked up life?"

I clutched my chest. This was escalating quickly. The fear in my eyes must have startled them both as they scrambled to composed themselves—for now.

"Kate, listen. This is confusing for both me and Liz." I tried to ease the situation.

"Thanks, Jason. I can speak for myself." Liz nodded at me with a look that told me to shut the fuck up or get the fuck out ... of my own shop ... which, for a split second, I seriously considered.

"I'm really sorry for your current situation. I really am. But can you put yourself in my shoes for a minute? Jason is my boyfriend. We were growing closer, and he was finally getting over you. You'd really torn his heart out when you left him. He *was* healing—at least, until you showed back up and turned things upside down again. How unfair is that to him? And me? Where does that leave me—the girlfriend—when the *soon-to-be ex*-wife is back in the picture?" Liz stared straight at Kate, who looked like she wanted to also run out of the door. Liz was about a foot taller than Kate, and when her feathers were ruffled, she looked to be four feet taller.

"I know. And I'm sorry. I fucked up. I don't know how many times I have to say it. I really, really fucked up. I'm paying for it, okay? It wasn't easy, coming back," Kate said.

"Then, why come back?" I butted back into the conversation.

Feelings and talking and confrontation and all that bullshit weren't my thing. At home, we didn't even say much to each other after she had told me about her Bosnian boyfriend. Our conversations were kept short and businesslike.

"You could have stayed gone and just let me live my life," I continued.

"I'm pregnant."

The silence that fell over us all was heavy as fuck, like one of those anxiety blankets. But it worked in reverse. Instead of calming us all down, it sent us into shock, though at least Kate looked like she had a weight off of her shoulders.

"Why didn't you say something sooner?" I asked, feeling suddenly dizzy. *Am I having a stroke?* At least I had a nurse with me.

I looked to Liz, who had gathered her things and was making her way out of the door while I was distracted by this new and fucked up information.

"Liz!" I ran after her. "Liz, please!"

I reached out to grab her as she turned toward me. I saw the tears in her eyes. She was gritting her teeth and doing everything she could to hold them back, but they were there.

"Handle your shit. I'm not going to play this side-bitch role anymore. I'm not a side-bitch, Jason. I'm a front-and-center bitch. You said so yourself! I was your front-and-center gal. Lately, I've been anything but!"

"You're not a side-bitch! How can you be? I'm not even really married!"

"Yes, you are."

"Can you just—"

"No—"

"But I—"

"No! And another thing, it was just an *internal* fart! Nothing came out of my ass!"

She marched to her car and sped off before I could even respond.

*Yeah, right. I've never heard an internal fart like that before.*

I stood there, dumbstruck and unable to move for what seemed like forever. I looked around me and out into the dark. The sun had gone down—literally. My sun, my star, was gone.

I turned to go back inside, suddenly furious with Kate.

"Why the fuck did you come here tonight? And why the fuck didn't you tell me that you're pregnant? What do you want from me?" I threw my hands in the air, fed up with her and myself.

I should have ended it the second she came back, but dumbass me had thought I was doing the right thing, and I wasn't. I'd screwed it all up. *Typical.*

"I came here tonight to give you the papers and tell you I'm gone. But when I saw *her*, I got a bit jealous. I don't know why. I guess I just realized what an idiot I am for giving you up. And now, I'm single and pregnant, and I caused another train wreck. I'm sorry, Jason. For everything. Here are the papers, and here's my contact information if you need anything else. I'm going back to Bosnia. I leave tonight. Tell Liz I'm sorry. Pregnancy hormones might have made me a tad moody."

"You can't make it single and pregnant in Bosnia! You don't have anything! How are you and the baby going to survive? Is Rico bitch face even the dad? You always told me you didn't even want kids!"

Kate flinched. She knew children had been a source of contention between us. I always wanted children, and she never wanted to be tied down. Except, I guessed, now, she was okay with being tied down—to a fucking hut in Bosnia.

"What the fuck? Yes, it's his. I'm not a whore, Jason! And I won't be returning to his *hut*. I did make friends over there, ya know. They are the ones who wired me the money to come back. They want me back. But I came back here because … because I thought I could make it work here, and maybe I even thought *we* could make it work, but I was only back a day before I remembered why I'd left in the first place!"

"Why did you leave in the first place? Besides the fact that Rico Suave whispered sweet little lies in your ear?"

"This just isn't the life I want to live. Blame it on my gypsy soul." She shrugged and vanished out the door.

At the beginning of the day, I'd had two women, and now, I only had Deuce. I cracked a beer open as soon as I came home and went to my firepit. The emotions I felt over whatever the hell had just happened poured out of me and onto paper. I wrote song after song after song before I realized they were about Liz. All of them. I loved her.

But true to my dumbass nature, I had fucked up.

If I was honest with myself, I had been confused about how I felt when I saw Kate in my shop that first time. I was happy, scared, angry, and also relieved that she was there. For an instant, my wife was back. Just seeing her had made my heart skip a beat. Though I would never be able to admit *that* part to Liz. I hadn't lied to Liz about my intentions. I never planned on getting back with Kate. I wasn't hopeful or anything for my marriage. I had truly only let Kate stay, so I could help her.

But I'd still felt something for Kate, slightly. What I now realized was that it wasn't love that I felt for Kate but care. Now that I remembered what love felt like—because I was head over boots in love with Liz—I knew I'd only *cared* for Kate when she came back. Sure, I had loved her once. A whole fucking lot. I'd searched high and low for her for years, and now, after she had left again, I only cared for her. I would always care for her even if I couldn't understand her gypsy ways. I wished her the best.

I sighed, reached down to pat Deuce on the head, and sang him my sob story. I was a fucking walking country song.

"Well, buddy, they're all gone. No more women for you—or me—to drool over and hump."

He leaned into my knee like he knew what I was saying. I always thought we connected on that level. As derpy as this dog was, he was also smart. He always knew when I was down because then he would be extra lovable.

*At least I have my dog*, I thought, which suddenly gave me a bright idea. Chicks liked dogs, and Liz liked Deuce, so … I snapped a picture of Deuce's lopsided grin and sent it over to Liz with a text.

> *Jason: Can we talk? I never thought that was a real fart, just so you know.*

I waited and waited and waited on her to text back. I paced around the patio, sang a few songs, drank another beer, and even made myself a charcuterie plate, to which Deuce gobbled up half.

*Look at me living the cultured life out here in the middle of nowhere in Nashvegas.*

I was up past my bedtime, waiting on that text back, and all of the excitement of the day had finally caught up to me. I dragged myself back inside and got ready for bed. I turned my ringer on my phone so that, in the very rare off chance that Liz would text back, I would hear it. But at this hour, I wasn't hopeful. I wasn't even hopeful she'd ever text me back. The thought of never seeing her beautiful face again had me, Jason Jones, on the verge of tears.

I had only cried two times in my life—that I would admit to anyway. One was when my best friend, Billy, from grade school had accidentally—on purpose—set a thumbtack in my chair before I went to sit down during homeroom one day. That hadn't been fun. The second time I'd cried was when I found out what had happened to Deuce—which, like I'd said, I didn't talk about. I hadn't even cried when Kate left.

Liz though ... when she had disappeared from my life with her fiery hair, her glitter boots, and her love of bacon, it killed me. She had come into my life like a flaming whirlwind of hope, desire, and romance. All dangerous things to a man, or anyone really, because those things could all be taken away so quickly—which left me where I was at now.

I lay back on my bed and bit down on my lip to keep it from quivering. I could handle this. Tomorrow would be a new day, and I had to keep on going even if, now, I was going it alone, without my sweet star.

My week was filled with interview after interview, but by the end of the week, I narrowed it down and built my team. Rob, of course, had come from Brad's place. He would be my manager. I trusted Rob, and he knew his stuff. Thankfully, I wouldn't have to train him much. I also stole two other employees from Brad's shop—another win for me. And I hired a handful of others who were experienced in the business of all things coffee and cooking.

Even without hearing from Liz, my week was starting to look up—slightly. The only thing I had left to do, which I'd been putting off, was to come up with a name for the shop. I should have had the signage already, but I struggled with that part. What was in a name? Everything. I racked my brain countless times, trying to figure out what I should call my shop, but it wasn't easy. It wasn't like I was writing a lyric. No, this had to be one, two, or three words that would make an impact. Something that was meaningful to me. I would come up with it soon enough; I had to.

In the meantime, I busied myself with even more gigs. I didn't turn down anything these days because money was tight. If I didn't start getting a steady income ASAP, I could lose everything I had put in this shop. All of my dreams would be up in flames, and I would have to crawl back to Brad. Yeah, right. I would never do that. I would take a job sniffing old men's armpits to test the effectiveness of deodorant before I would ever work for that wack-job Brad again.

*Ding.*

My phone went off in my pocket. I pathetically kept my ringer on in case Liz ever decided to answer my last text. How could anyone not answer a text photo of a cute Deuce? Maybe I shouldn't have mentioned the fart. I meant ... the *internal fart.* I would give my left nut to have Liz lie next to me, internal fart or not. I didn't care. I just wanted her back in my arms—and in my bed. Also on my cock and in my mouth.

I checked my phone. It was her. I mentally prepared myself before I read her text.

I paced the floor of the shop, trying to guess what she would say to me after nearly a week of ignoring my text. Ghosted me. She'd ghosted me! That was familiar. So, now, what could she possibly say to get me to text her back? Maybe *Jason, I need your hard cock again?* Yeah, that would work.

My dick suddenly woke and throbbed in my pants. I hadn't even rubbed one out this week—that was how distraught I'd been. I patted my zipper and promised my pecker I would take care of him later. I had to be brave and check her text first.

*How did I let a woman get to me like this? Oh, yeah, I love her. Is she going to say she loves me too?*

That thought helped. I was now brave *and* motivated. Liz was going to tell me she loved me too, and we'd ride off into the sunset. The Nashville sunset—on that rooftop bar that she liked. That was the plan. I convinced myself of it before I tapped my phone, and her message appeared.

*Liz: Tomorrow, will you be at the shop around lunch? I was going to stop by for a quick second.*

I wasted no time in responding. I didn't care how desperate I looked at this point. I ached for Liz, no matter why she wanted to stop by—which, again, I convinced myself it was a good thing. She wanted to set things right—for our future. *I think?*

*Me: Yep. I'll be here. You can count on me! Can't wait to see you.*

I read my response again and again. My text might have sounded a little too happy, a little too hopeful, a little too pathetic. I was overthinking things, and I guessed Liz was probably doing the same thing. Except she had Jess—Team Jizz. I wondered if they were together now, problem-solving the situation and analyzing my texts.

*Me: Would you like lunch? Can I pick you up anything to eat while you're here? I promise, no hot chicken.*

I tried to continue the conversation. Just getting that text from Liz made me smile into my phone like an idiot. All week, I had been a big sourpuss, but one *ding* from Liz, and I now felt on top of the world.

*Liz: No, thanks. I'm meeting up with Jess for lunch. See you tomorrow!*

I nodded at my phone as if she could see my response. At least we were talking now.

# 13

**LIZ**

I opened his shop's door to a ringing of bells.

"New bells?" I looked up, trying to find what had ousted my arrival.

"Yeah, do you like them? I think it gives the shop a classic feel. Also, it might warn me if any crazies are coming in."

"Like me? Warning: redhead alert!"

"I didn't say it would warn me if any hot chicks were coming in, but that is a million-dollar idea that someone needs to get on!" He grinned at me.

His dazzling smile made my breath catch in my throat and stopped me in my tracks. I started to second-guess the reason I was here—to officially let him go.

I walked around the shop in silence, not knowing what to say or how to start.

"It looks really great in here! You still set to open soon?"

"In exactly six weeks. Opening day is October 23. I've got a few gigs lined up, and we will be having one big party that evening after the ribbon-cutting. I hope you can come. You did help me with all of this." He motioned around the room toward the tables I'd picked out, the art I'd picked out, and the Edison bulbs that hung above the bar that I'd told him he absolutely had to have.

"October 23, eh? I would love to, but I'm not sure that's a good idea." I pulled out a chair and sat down, patting the seat next to me.

"Here we go again. You want me to sit down, so this can't be good." He dragged his feet toward me and weakly pulled out a chair. "How's work? How have you been this week?"

"You're not changing the subject! Such a Jason thing to do!" I teased, missing him already.

*I can do this. I can do this. I can do this. I have to do this. Don't I?*

"She's gone, Liz. Kate left right after you did. She only came by to drop off the signed divorce papers, and then she flew back to Bosnia." He leaned back in his chair and ran his hands through his sexy, disheveled hair.

"Really? Bosnia? And pregnant? How is she going to—" I scratched my head.

"I don't know. Not my problem."

"Hmm."

"Does that change why you came here?"

"I don't think so." I sighed.

"I was afraid of that. I know you have your mind made up. I just want to apologize for putting you through all of this. I should have figured out the divorce proceedings long ago, but truth be told, I wasn't over her until you came along. I didn't have the motivation to do what needed to be done, but you … you lit a fire under my ass. Literally! Remember the hot chicken?"

"I do." I laughed as I glanced toward the bar, where we had set each other's loins on fire.

"Have you had hot chicken since then?"

He reached over and playfully squeezed my knee. I immediately felt the electric tingles, and by the look on his face, he felt it too. I shook my head, afraid to speak. If I opened my mouth now, I was going to cry. I'd spent the last week going back and forth on why or why not I should give him another chance. My brain told me that he needed time to heal, but my heart said—well, screw that bitch; I couldn't listen to her. She had gotten me in trouble so many times before. So, this time, I listened to my brain. She was kind of a badass anyway.

"I appreciate you. I like you a lot—maybe too much. This last week was hard for me. I've been upset about Kate, and I had this story built up in my head that you and her were living together and raising the baby as your own."

Jason gasped, which made me feel even dumber for the bullshit stories I told myself sometimes. Maybe my brain wasn't such a badass after all.

"I know; I know," I continued. "I think, in a way, I had to tell myself something like that to protect myself. It's easier for me to let go if I'm mad. But you really didn't do anything wrong. Yes, I wish you hadn't let her back in your life, but that wasn't fair of me to even wish that because you were family. Even if, in my opinion, she is a coldhearted bitch, she was still legally married to you. She was still … your wife," I choked the words out. I hated saying that she was his wife.

"Jeez. No! I wish you had told me you thought that. Now, I feel terrible! I never meant to hurt anyone, Liz. Especially you. I wish I had cut her off too. I made a mistake. A big one. And it cost me—you. Whatever it was that we had, it just happened so fast. It took me by surprise. I was really beginning to know you, and I liked that. I more than like you."

*What does that mean, he more than likes me? Does he love me?*

I sucked in my breath and held it, clenching my jaw to stop myself from ugly-crying.

"I don't want to distract from any of the work you need to do to fully get over her."

"What if I'm already over her?"

"You aren't."

"Why do you say that? That's not true."

"Because that's what I need to tell myself—for me. I don't want to get hurt twice."

"You won't."

"How do I know? You know … and I can't even believe I'm going to say this, but … I more than like you too. The whirlwind romance swept me off of my feet. You were everything I wanted in a man that I could see myself settling down with, except you had that one little issue. You were married! But what did I do? I did what I always do; I let myself fall. But this time, I didn't grow hot and cold or push you away. I believed in it—in us. I stayed and tried and told myself I would give it a go, but I would still be on guard. I wasn't on guard. I fell hard. I'm still on the fucking ground actually."

"Me too. I'm down in the pits. And you are *the* woman I want to settle down with and give this relationship thing another shot. But I understand. You are scared and letting go. I did hurt you. It wasn't intentional, and I really did believe that just because I was married on a piece of paper and my wife hadn't been around for years … I mean, hell, what if she were dead and gone? I don't know what I was trying to say. I didn't go about things the right way. I'm sorry. That's what I'm trying to say. I'm just so damn sorry."

"Me too."

I grabbed my things to go, unsure if I could make it out the door before wailing. He'd said he more than liked me. He'd said she left. He'd said he wanted to settle down with me.

*So, why am I leaving again?*

"Wait! So, this is it? You really don't want to start over? This week has been hell without you. I'm not even myself! Are you sure this is what you want? Because if you truly want this and you truly feel this way, I will leave you alone." He stood up in front of me, blocking my path toward the door.

His eyes looked like they were about to spill over, and I felt like shit. Typical Liz moment.

"Don't you know that girls never know what they want?"

*There. I gave him a sliver of hope. Or did I give me a sliver of hope?*

"I've got to go," I whispered as he inched closer toward me.

The provocative scent of his familiar cologne sent me right back to that night on the dance floor. I'd caught a whiff of that scent two days ago on a patient I was caring for in the hospital. Let's just say, I cared for that patient a lot—like a whole lot. I had checked that man's blood pressure probably forty-two times.

*Thump, thump, thump. Squeeze and squeeze. Here we go again.*

"I'll see you around, Liz." He reached his hand out to me but stopped short, letting it fall to his side.

What I wouldn't give for him to touch me. Just one more electric touch of his, and I would probably throw my arms around him and ask him to marry me. But he didn't. He let me go.

I nodded in answer, not trusting my voice to speak. I couldn't even look up at his eyes. I just had to leave—and quickly. I turned to walk my Jell-O legs out the door and felt his gaze watch me go.

I didn't remember my drive back to work, and even though I'd done everything that Team Jizz had discussed over lunch, I was still a hot, tearful mess. Jess had told me to remember the pain I felt.

"Focus on the pain," she'd said.

I had to focus on what I had felt when I saw Kate walk through that door to his shop. But truth be told, I hadn't told anyone what I'd felt when I saw her walk through the door. I recognized her now. Those long, dark locks and those scared, darting eyes. When she had told Jason she was pregnant, I had known that it wasn't her first pregnancy.

I'd dealt with Kate before, years ago. I wasn't even sure she had been with Jason at the time. I just knew she had been in the clinic I worked for. It had been my first job, and I would always remember the terror on her face as she repeatedly asked if the procedure was confidential. She hadn't wanted anyone to know, especially her boyfriend—as, according to her, the baby wasn't his.

I wasn't one to judge. I didn't know if it had been Jason's baby or not, and I hoped to never know that information. Even if I knew, it was none of my business, and laws prevented me from telling it anyway. So, when I had recognized her face walking through that door, I'd at least tried to be friendly. I had known she wasn't innocent, but she was also a human. That didn't mean I still couldn't stand her.

"You're not a side bitch," Jess had reminded me.

I had repeated it all the way to the café, musing over if saying positive affirmations really worked to make us better people—or not. I never had the patience to keep at it. Did I feel like a front-and-center bitch? Not when Kate had walked through that door. And that was why I had to let him go. I knew myself and my worth. I valued myself. I had only been hypnotized by magic dick. His magic dick.

I parked my car in the hospital garage and leaned into the steering wheel to relive what had happened before I had to go in and pretend I was anything other than a miserable mess right now. Jason had said he more than liked me and that I was someone he could settle with. And then I'd given him that sliver of hope.

*Why did I give him, or me, that sliver of hope?*

I made my way into work and busied myself so that the rest of the day went by in a blur. My coworkers offered shoulders to cry on and Doritos and Cokes out of the vending machine. They knew my love language—junk food. My team's efforts were sweet, but nothing could erase or even soften the loss I now carried. Not even stuffing my face with processed crap.

"Do I need to rough him up a bit? Take my scalpel and cut off his left nipple?" my boss asked.

"That was my favorite nipple!" I moaned.

"You want it? I'll give it to you. You can tack it up on your front door as a warning to others."

"Jeez! What are you, one of those serial killer doctors?" I sucked in my breath and took a step back.

"I might have watched one too many horror movies, growing up. Probably explains a lot," she mused.

"Is there anything you can do to make me forget? Morphine? Vicodin? Lobotomy? Can you rip him from my memory? Like it … like *he* never happened?"

"Oh, honey. I wish it were that easy. I can give you some really bad advice that might help. But only if you want it."

"Anything. I'll do anything at this point."

"Don't you know that the best way to get over someone is to get under someone?"

"Does that really work?"

"Yes. A distraction. But it's kind of like jumping from the fire and into the frying pan. Now, I'm not saying that sleeping with someone else is doctor's orders, but do it anyway. Put yourself back out there—ASAP."

"Doctor's orders: go get laid. Got it," I repeated, nodding in agreement.

It wasn't exactly a bad idea. If it worked, Jason would be out of my life, and I would be on to the next dude—a more available guy.

*But what if I never have that spark again? What if that electric tingle is only something Jason can do to me? What if I never feel like I felt when I was with him? What am I going to do without his biceps, his songs, his magic dick?*

I didn't have answers, and I knew I wouldn't get answers. Dr. Bailey was right. I needed a distraction. I needed to meet someone that would take Jason's place even if that was an impossible role to fill because who the hell would ever hand me a jar of stars again? That was the single most romantic thing anyone had ever done for me. If men like that were really out there, I needed to find them. So far, my track record on romantic men was one to … twenty-three or something.

I texted Jess.

> *Me: Let's go out tonight? I need a distraction.*

> *Jess: What do you mean, a distraction? You mean, you want to make another bad decision?*

> *Me: Yes.*

> *Jess: Let's do it.*

"I can't believe Dr. Bailey told you that!" Jess said from the front seat of the car.

Her husband was playing chauffeur again even though I didn't plan on drinking tonight. I needed to be sober and have my wits about me as I searched for a clone of Jason. My pits started to sweat as I realized what I was up against—special Jason versus the world of assholes I was used to. I held up my arms, airing them out, and sighed.

"She said it was the doctor's orders. That I needed a distraction."

"And she didn't think distracting yourself with healthier alternatives, like yoga and mindfulness, would help? Just hot sex with hot dudes?" Luke asked. His gaze met mine in the rearview mirror.

"Whatever works. And fast," I answered.

"Wanna know what I think? You want a man's opinion on the whole situation?"

Jess groaned and reached over to squeeze her husband's knee. "Now's not the time, honey. I'm sure Liz can figure it out … with my help, of course! You know we don't do the mansplain thing."

"Wait a minute. Let's see what he has to say. Maybe I do want a man's opinion. What say you, Luke?"

His brows pulled together.

"I say you two both made mistakes. I mean, sure, he should have turned Kate away as soon as he saw her, but can you really blame him? She'd disappeared years ago without any answers. He deserved to get those answers, and he let her stay to *help* her. He told you there wasn't anything going on between them. He kept up communications with you. I really feel like he was doing all he could and got stuck in between two women. He just didn't handle it well. Do you have any idea how hard it is to please one woman, let alone two?"

Jess shifted in her seat. This wouldn't be the first time Luke and I had bantered, but I could tell by the way Jess kept quiet—unusual for her—that she agreed with him.

"But that's the thing. He shouldn't have tried to please her. She walked out on him. He should have just—"

"Step back for a second. What would you have done in that situation? If your husband suddenly came back and looked like he needed your help? Never mind. Don't answer that," Luke said, aware that his train of thought was derailing.

Jess snorted. "Liz would have told him to fuck off."

"Yeah, I get that." Luke shook his head and sighed. "Well ... what I'm trying to say is, I think Jason is a good guy, from what you've told me. I think he was in a bad situation and tried to make the best of it. I think you overreacted a bit too quickly. Maybe even pushed him a little bit."

"Whoa, whoa, whoa!" Jess shouted.

My eyes grew wide as her husband called me out on my bullshit. I had been so wrapped up in my feelings that maybe I acted too quickly. If I hadn't then, why had I given Jason—I mean, myself—that sliver of hope? Maybe I had been *too* extra, demanding his attention—all of it.

"It's okay, Jess. As much as I don't like to admit it, I think Luke might be right. But just a little," I said as I cringed in my seat. "I think I was hurt that Kate came back, and he just let her into his life again so easily. I know it wasn't his fault. I just wish he'd handled her differently. I just wish he'd picked me."

"But he did pick you. He told you that. The only thing he didn't do was kick his clearly fucked up wife out on the streets. Now, maybe you would be able to do that because you are headstrong, but maybe Jason isn't. Maybe he truly does have a heart of gold. Not all of us men are assholes, ya know."

"You think I'm an asshole for not putting up with people's shit?" I asked.

This conversation was a total mood killer. I didn't even want to go out and find a distraction anymore.

"Not at all. I think it's a great quality to be able to be that up-front with people and know your boundaries. I admire that about you and Jess. Both of y'all are strong in that way. But—"

"But what?" Jess turned in her seat to face her husband.

The tension in the air was stifling. I cracked a window and tried to steady my breathing.

"But … stubbornness. Y'all can be so damn stubborn."

Jess looked back at me, and we both grinned. Luke had hit the nail on the head. We were stubborn as fuck. She and I both knew it, accepted it, and wore it as a badge of honor. Sometimes, that was a good quality, but sometimes, like now, it was a bad one.

Luke caught the subtle exchange between Team Jizz.

"See, y'all know it! Women … ugh," he groaned.

"So, now, what do you suggest? You're saying I fucked up, right? But he fucked up too, yeah?" I asked.

"You both fucked up. I don't think either of you intended to hurt one another. Shit just happens. He tried to make it right, and you were too stubborn to let him. You wanted things done on your watch and your way. The world doesn't always work like that. No matter how much you try to force it. People just handle their bullshit in their own way. So, what I suggest is, you recognize that you also could have handled things differently, and when you find this distraction you're after tonight, maybe try to keep an open mind … ya know, in case his long-lost wife comes back and he tries to remedy the situation while holding on to you. Fuck, that's a damn soap opera. The drama! The drama! How about you start by making wiser choices? I'm not trying to be an asshole, but I'm just saying to get your head in the game. No more bad decisions—or at least, don't make as many of them."

We pulled up to Broadway where Luke usually let us out, but neither Jess nor I moved. I didn't feel like going out anymore, and by Jess's exhausted expression, she didn't either.

"I don't think I can do this," I muttered. My palms were sweaty, and I just wanted to crawl back into bed. I was feeling like a really big asshole at the moment. "Damn it, Luke, why do you have to make so much sense? You just ruined my night."

Jess nodded her head. "It's why I married him. He does make sense sometimes. We balance each other out." She reached over to pat his knee again as he leaned into her and pecked her on the cheek.

"Team Jizz has gone limp. I repeat, Team Jizz has gone limp. It is time for some Luscious Luke to the rescue!" Luke cupped his hand to his mouth as if speaking through a microphone.

"Luscious Luke?" I shuddered. "Sure, whatever. Let's just go have fun—without being on the hunt for a distraction. No more bad decisions, right? I feel like shit now anyway. Thanks, Luke!"

"I'm sorry. I'll make it up to y'all. Come on, let's go." He turned the car around and headed in the other direction.

I didn't know where we were going, and I didn't even care. My thoughts were no longer on a sexy distraction but on the crappy way I now felt. I kept catching both Jess and her husband's gaze in the mirror. They were checking to see if I was crying. I wasn't, but I sure as hell wanted to. I had never felt like a bigger asshole before in my life.

*This self-awareness crap is bullshit.*

I had put up my walls *and* steel-reinforced them to protect myself, but the only trouble with that was that I had blocked Jason out completely, and he didn't deserve it. My actions might have protected me, but they caused him pain, which I didn't want to do. I wasn't a little star. I was a fucking supernova, whirling through bad decision after bad decision until I collapsed and disappeared, leaving everyone scratching their heads and wondering, *What the hell just happened?* I knew what Jason would say—*Redheads.*

# 14

**JASON**

Deuce's. That was what I had settled on for my shop name. The one constant in my life was my farty dog, Deuce. So, in honor of his awesomeness, Deuce's was set to open this weekend.

Beyond excited, I couldn't even describe how I'd felt the moment that sign was put up outside. I'd even had a small photoshoot for him—for marketing, of course. The flyers I had sent out for the grand opening had a picture of Deuce as he slept beside my guitar. What a lazy turd! But it had worked because I'd already had several people call and inquire about details, times, dates, gigs.

I planned on playing the first thirty minutes, and then after me and my thank-you to everyone, I had booked several other friends, all much more badass than me. The best part: I'd made it a charity night. Not only would I be taking donations for the local animal shelters, but I would also donate ten percent of proceeds to them as well. I'd even been on the radio to discuss it! Talk about surreal!

My weekend was going to be amazing, which I really needed after my last few weeks of misery. Liz had reached out to me to apologize shortly after that night she had walked out, but we still hadn't seen each other or even planned to. She'd said, in her own words, *I fucked up*. I didn't think she'd fucked up, but had she been a bit hard on me? Of course. She was a redhead. I didn't expect any different. I had known what I was getting into when I first slapped her ass and told her to call me Mr. Jones. It could have been worse. She could have broken into my home and woven me a shit blanket.

We had been *cordial* with each other. We'd only spoken a handful of times since she left, and most of our texts had been short and centered around the shop. She was staying busy with her job. I suspected for the same reasons I was staying busy with mine— to create a distraction. When my mind was busy with training new employees, it couldn't wonder what she was doing.

*Is she smiling? Is she laughing? Is she as sad as I am?*

I didn't want Liz sad. I'd almost … almost reached out to her several times to talk about feelings. But in the end, I left her alone. She had told me that she dealt with things in her own way, and I wanted to let her. I had, however, texted her Deuce's grand-opening flyer. It was only fair that she knew about the celebration, seeing as though she had helped me with so much. She had finally responded three days later.

*Liz: Congratulations! So cute.*

I tapped my chin, wondering what those few words had meant. Did that mean she was coming, or not?

I hoped she would at least come by to see what the place looked like as an up-and-running business. I wanted her to see the industrial look that she had put together and that everyone who had stopped by raved and raved about. A lot in the shop had been inspired by her. I even had a glittered piece of artwork—a gold star—hanging behind the bar, right where she had tacked up my to-do list, which was now complete.

"Hey, boss! Where do you want me to put these boxes?" Rob said as he peeked inside my tiny back office, which was really supposed to be a closet.

I barely had elbow room in here, but it was a space that I could use to be alone and think … of Liz … and more boring stuff, like boxes.

"You don't have to call me that, ya know. Just set them in the hall. I'll bring them around back before I leave. How's the kitchen coming along? Everyone know what they are doing now? Are you able to handle it, or do I need to step in?" I asked.

"Honestly, I don't think you could have picked better employees. They all seem to know what they're doing, so I haven't had much to do with them at all. I think they got this. I think *you* got this!" He stuck his hand out for a fist bump.

Rob tried to keep my mind off of Liz whenever he caught me drifting into space. Whether it was because he didn't want another mishap with the steamer or because he truly cared, I didn't know. He was here for me though, and for that, I was grateful.

Plus, he helped me so damn much with the employees. I'd found out I was over my head with all of that, but Rob had come to the rescue. Brad, on the other hand, had been nowhere in sight. Good riddance!

"Thanks, man. I think *we* got this. Did you get to try anything on the menu? I know they are testing a few of the items out this week."

"I did! The chicken-and-waffle thing! You know that one with the fried egg inside a hole in a waffle and Nashville hot chicken on top? We called that a Toad in the Hole when I was a kid, but I like your name better—Fire in the Hole! Where did you get that idea anyway? I didn't know you were that smart!" Rob teased.

"Oh, I don't know. It just came to me, I guess," I lied as he shrugged his shoulders and went back to work.

I wouldn't be able to order anything on my menu without remembering her. The fancy flower omelet was on the menu. A charcuterie plate was on the menu. Bacon, too, was on the menu, of course.

I put my elbows on my desk and rested my head in my hands. Whenever my eyes closed, if I concentrated hard enough, I could still see Liz's smile. Though it was slowly fading now. I hadn't seen her in so long that my memories were still there but blurred as if someone had taken a sponge and glossed over the details. Not all of the details. I still could remember the way her tits had bounced while she rode me like a rocket ship. My cock thickened, just from thinking about that.

I so wished she'd come to opening night. I needed to catch a whiff of that sweet peaches and cream she always smelled like. That scent brought me back to the dance floor, the bedroom, the firepit. Those memories were stuck but fading. I needed to remember. I needed to see her even if she just stood in the back and refused to talk to me. I wanted her there. I *needed* her there. The past few weeks had eaten me alive, and keeping all of this emotion inside of me was killing me. Maybe, just maybe, if she were there, we could talk. And maybe, just maybe, I could sing for her, a very special song I'd been working on.

The silver lining of my break from Liz, even though I firmly believed in saying *fuck silver linings*, was that I had been able to pour my heart and soul into my music. Whenever I wasn't busy in the shop, that was. I had written twelve songs and counting. One of which I would perform on opening night. I wasn't that confident in my writing ability—*yet*—so my customers were about to be my test subjects in every way. Coffee, tunes, and bacon—the way to Liz's heart. Minus the cocktails. It was too late for me to get a liquor license after all.

Opening day was here, and I was scared shitless. I hadn't even slept the night before or the night before that or the night before that. I was about to have the biggest day of my life, my dream come true, and yet Liz still took up all the space in my brain. No matter how busy I'd kept myself, Liz was always there. She had never told me if she would be at the grand-opening celebration tonight or not, so I didn't get my hopes up.

But just in case she did decide to show up, I already had a speech and a song planned just for her. I felt like I'd apologized fifteen hundred times by now, but it would never be enough for Liz *or* me. Just an apology wouldn't do her justice. Nope, not Liz. Liz was *extra* whether she liked to admit it or not. It was one of the things I loved about her. She had brought charcuterie into my life. How could I not love that?

The only way I could make this work would be if I could be that something—or someone—extra she needed. She had told me that she wasn't sure what she wanted, which left the door open for me to get my shit together and show her that I could be what she wanted. I had made a mistake. A big fucking mistake. And, now, that mistake was back in Bosnia, and I would never see her again. I wasn't even sad about that anymore. Kate wasn't meant to be, but Liz … Liz was my soul mate.

I didn't know how else to explain the chemistry between us. Those tingles we both felt when our bodies brushed up against each other? That was our souls talking. I know; I know. Jason Jones was getting into the feels. Deep into the feels. Macho man with that tatted-up arm was showing his *feelings*. Damn right. I'd been doing a little self-reflecting, a little growing. I *might* have picked up a few books in the Self-Help section. I wanted to tell Liz how I felt. I just didn't know how. I had so much to learn, but I was making slow progress.

*Better than no progress*, I reminded myself.

It was so easy for my feelings to pour out on paper and in song, but speaking them? That shit was hard. If I had told Liz how I felt and been up-front and honest about how I had struggled to get over Kate, I probably wouldn't be alone right now. Maybe she would have worked through all those things with me if I had just communicated it.

Instead, I had tried to juggle both women and play like things were okay. I knew they weren't okay. That hadn't stopped me from trying to force it to be okay. I never should have expected Liz to still be with me while my wife was back. What the hell had I been thinking? It was the feelings thing, the emotions. I never got in tune with them. But, now, I was working on it. I did know the emotion I felt was love—for Liz, if that wasn't clear. I knew I had been in a shit triangle. It did get confusing.

But like I'd said, my emotions came out in song, and tonight, I hoped to sing them to Liz, *if* she decided to show up. I couldn't blame her if she didn't.

"So far, so good, boss!" Rob clapped me on the back.

"Dude. It's Jason. I'm not anything like Brad. You don't have to address me as boss. I'm not one of those regular bosses. I'm a *cool* boss." I made finger guns and clicked my tongue.

"Cool … yeah …" Rob nodded. "Just don't do that finger-gun thing if Liz shows up."

"So, you're saying—"

"I know that's what you've been thinking about. It's obvious when you're in Liz Land. You get this far-off gaze, your mouth hangs open, and sometimes, I think you might even drool. I know you haven't been here today. I mean, you're here, but your mind isn't. Your mind is still with her. Notice how I won't let you get near the espresso machine? I don't need you burning yourself again," Rob said, folding his arms and waiting on me to respond.

I didn't know I was that obvious of a mess.

"Really? I drool? Sheesh. My mind *is* on her. I think if she doesn't show up tonight, that will give me the answer I've been waiting on—if she is still interested or not. Maybe after tonight, I can get some closure. Damn if I'm not always looking for closure."

I headed back to my office while business was slow. The official party wouldn't kick off until four more hours, and then I would perform shortly after. I never got stage fright anymore, but tonight, I thought I might need to sneak a shot of whiskey before I sang. Not only was I performing my Liz song, but it was also *my* song—the first one I had ever written and would sing in public. People were going to love it or hate it.

I busied myself with paperwork, which was really difficult for me. I hated sitting down in front of a computer or at a desk. Spreadsheets and e-mails? Fuck that. Which was why I chose to do it for the next few hours. I needed something to take up some time while I put my head in the game. I went over inventory about twenty times, printed off two new recipes, filed some important legal documents that I didn't understand, and uploaded a few pictures of Deuce to the official Deuce's social media accounts. His social media profiles were surprisingly popular, even more so than mine. Everyone loved an ugly dog.

I stretched my legs and stood up at T-minus one hour to go. The ribbon-cutting had been earlier this morning, thankfully, so all I really needed to do was play host and coordinate the gigs. I closed my eyes and took a deep breath.

*That's T-minus one hour until I might see her beautiful face again.*

# LIZ

I couldn't believe Jess had talked me into this. I hadn't seen Jason since I left this place. I purposely avoided Broadway and anywhere that he might be for a gig—or a girl. I had been in such a fog these last few weeks, avoiding him so that I could handle some of my own bullshit. I'd even found a therapist—for Ayesha. Just kidding. Therapy was for Liz and all of my personalities. I knew I made bad decisions, and I had trouble letting *the right* people past my walls. But after Luke's heartfelt, mansplaining, come-to-Jesus meeting he had with me in the car, something needed to change.

Who would have ever thought it would be my best friend's husband who would be the man to change my life—for the better? That sounded like some kinky shit, but it wasn't. Luke had made me see, after all these years, that maybe I had also sorta slightly—I cringed when I had to admit this—been an asshole too. Maybe it hadn't always been the men in my life who were tough to crack. *I* was tough to crack.

*Yay therapy.*

I didn't want to be tough to crack anymore—not with Jason especially, which was why I had avoided him, up until now at least. He had been open and honest with me, which was more than most men in my life had done. I also didn't want to make bad decisions anymore, not with men anyway. Team Jizz still had a green light. Always.

So, I had that going for me, self-awareness and all. It had been a slow process, but I was healing. I thought that by the time I was seventy-eight, I should be fully healed and have this life thing figured out, and maybe then I could let Jason in and not be so guarded.

At least, that had been the plan until I showed Jess and Luke the grand-opening invitation for Deuce's.

*"You still have that sliver of hope there, Ms. Live the Life You Love?" Luke asked me.*

*Okay, so my therapy might have been wearing off on my friends too. Positive thinking, right? We only had this one life to live and yada, yada, yada.*

*"Living my best life, Luke. I'm a work in progress." I cringed. "The sliver of hope never left."*

*"Great. Because you need to go to this. Talk to him in person and maybe get some closure—or just see where the conversation takes you. Give him a key to your fortress. Tell him you are slowly dismantling it. And apologize—again." Jess tossed me the invitation.*

*"Okay," I said.*

So, remember when I had said that I couldn't believe she'd talked me into going? That was a lie. I had been easily talked into going. Like I'd said, I was a *slow* work in progress.

We stepped through the door to Deuce's and into a crowd. There wasn't an empty table in sight. I scanned the room for Jason, who I found working behind the counter. I saw his biceps first, and then I saw that dazzling smile of his as he looked up and met my eyes.

*Thump, thump, thump. Squeeze, squeeze, squeeze.*

I grabbed Jess's elbow to hold me steady while he practically floated over to me. He looked so happy, and I was glad to see that. He deserved this dream of his to come true. It really did look amazing in here, and by the laughter and energy in the room, I guessed his customers were happy too.

"Liz! You came!"

Jason threw his arms around me in a tight embrace, and I instantly melted. I wanted to tell him to please not let go, but I was aware of everyone around me, and that seemed to be another one of those bad decisions.

*Stupid therapy.*

"Jason! This place looks amazing! You did so well," I said, pulling back from the safety of his arms.

"*We.* You helped, little star. Look! I even put up a gold star just for you, right alongside the to-do list. It even has *glitter* on it!" He pointed toward the star that hung on the wall.

It was so me, and I absolutely loved it.

"Oh my! You did!" I gushed.

Luke cleared his throat next to me, bringing me and Jason back down to reality.

"Oh, I'm sorry! Jason, this is Luke, Jess's husband. And of course, you know Jess. Team Jizz!"

"I've heard a lot about you, Luke! You are so lucky to have Team Jizz in your life."

Jason stuck out his hand to greet Luke, and he even hugged Jess. I watched her hands brush lightly against his biceps as she winked at me from behind his back.

"They are … something. That's for sure. I've heard a lot about you too. You seem to be the most popular artist on Broadway these days. Do we get to hear you play tonight?" Luke asked.

"You do. Actually … shit. That's in just a few minutes." Jason glanced around the room. "I'm afraid I don't see any tables, but if y'all come up to the bar area, I can grab you some drinks and menus real quick before I have to get up there and do my thing."

Luke and Jess nodded as we made our way to the back. I felt a hand grab me and pull me to the side. I already knew by the tingle that shot up my arm that it was Jason.

He leaned down to whisper in my ear, "Thank you for coming."

His soft breaths sent a tickle straight down to my crotch. I needed to apologize to him, have the talk, and then hopefully get that fuck up against the wall that I'd wanted for forever now.

"I wouldn't have missed it," I whispered back as I met his gaze. I still had ahold of his hand.

"You'll be glad you didn't. I think. Gotta run!" he said as he disappeared into the crowd.

*What exactly did he mean by that?*

I searched out Jess and Luke and squeezed in beside them.

"He still likes you." Jess smirked at me.

"Oh no, he doesn't. He more than likes her. Did you not see the look in his eyes when he put his arms around her? I don't know who has it worse, Liz—you or him. Y'all need to talk—and fuck."

"Agreed," I sighed as I fanned myself. It was getting hot in here.

"Hey there, everyone! If I can have your attention, please! I wanted to thank everyone for coming out tonight." Jason was on the stage.

This was the first time I had seen him onstage since the Mr. Jones night. Any other time he had sang had been directly to me. I suddenly had a sense of déjà vu as I watched him work the audience.

"This place has been a dream of mine for so long, and it couldn't have happened without your support, so thank you all! I also want to introduce you to the famous Deuce himself. He is my six-year-old adopted BFF. He is ugly as all get-out because he was involved in a very bad bar fight. He won, of course. Say hello to Deuce and also to my amazing manager who I couldn't run this shop without—Rob!"

Jason stepped back as Rob carried Deuce out in his arms. I giggled to myself, knowing that Rob had to hold Deuce so that he didn't run off and pee everywhere.

The crowd applauded and whistled at Deuce—or Jason. He was dazzling up there in the limelight. Mesmerizing even. I was sure his grin alone would make regular customers out of all these women here tonight.

"Thank you. Thank you," he said as the crowd grew quiet. "Don't forget that, tonight, we are taking donations for the local animal shelters and also ten percent of proceeds go toward benefiting the shelter that Deuce had called home for far too long."

The crowd cheered, and I was starting to feel boxed in. There was barely breathing room, let alone standing room. Mostly hot college girls, of course, but it was a decent mix. I even spotted my coworkers mingling in a corner.

"Last, but definitely not least—and she might hate me for this—but I want to thank the woman who helped me pull this place together. I mean, look around you, everyone. Did she do an amazing job or what? She put her style into all of this. Her *extra-special* style. Give it up for Liz." His eyes locked on mine.

Jess jumped up and down beside me, clapping in my ear. Even Luke hooted and pulled me in for a hug. I was pretty sure my face was as red as that time he had brought me up onstage. At least that shit wouldn't be happening again.

"Come on up here, Liz!" Jason motioned for me to come toward him, patting the seat beside him.

It wasn't like I could hide. All eyes in the room had turned to face me. It was my move now. I made my way through the crowd, trying to calm myself before I had to look at all of them from atop the stage.

*Fucking hell. He is so getting an earful after this. Living my best life, living my best life, living my best life.*

"What are you doing?" I whispered through a fake smile as soon as I was within earshot of him.

"Being extra. Sit," he gently commanded.

I wasn't going to lie. I liked that. His command sent me right back to Mr. Jones Land, so I happily—okay, I nervously—obliged. I clutched the edge of the seat with my hands, so I wouldn't fall off. Whatever the hell was about to happen, I wasn't sure if my poor heart could handle it. It felt like it was about to beat right out of my chest and run out of the door, never to be seen again.

"Are y'all ready for some music?" he called out.

The crowd cheered, as usual. Everyone loved Jason—everyone. I sighed.

"Well, let's get this party started! This song is my first song that I ever wrote and will perform in public. It was inspired by someone who told me that she would never let herself be anything other than a front-and-center bitch. I know, I know, right? Girl problems. It comes with the guitar. Anywho, I want to acknowledge that this fine lady was and never will be second rate. Hopefully, she'll know that by the end of this song."

He side-eyed me with that panty-melting grin of his. The crowd was quietly murmuring, no doubt about this drama that Jason Jones was about to publicly air onstage. I bit my lip until I tasted blood. If this was his version of *extra*, I was going to have to give him *extra* ass-kickings. If there was a loony Liz reference or anything of the sort in this damn song, I might cut him up into those stars we'd talked about.

I looked over at him as he started to sing. I couldn't catch my break enough to smile or pout. I was in a state of shock. Stupid Jason Jones shock.

*Fucking hell, I think I'm about to get roasted.*

# KAT ADDAMS

*Fireflies in my sky,*
*A touch that electrifies.*
*It's you.*
*Oh, that's all you.*

*Flaming hair and eyes of blue,*
*Please let me prove*
*That I'm through.*
*She's gone,*
*And you're my number one.*
*You're*
*My*
*Front-and-center*
*Bitch.*

*Fancy pants, wanna dance?*
*Your breath is mine.*
*Let's take a chance.*
*It's true.*
*I'd do it all for you.*

*Your sweet peach on my lips,*
*The way you tease me,*
*With them hips,*
*It's true.*
*I've fallen in love*
*With you.*

*Flaming hair and eyes of blue,*
*Please let me prove*
*that I'm through.*
*She's gone,*
*And you're my number one.*
*You're*
*My*
*Front-and-center*
*Bitch.*

*Sparkle boots and*
*Internal toots.*
*We drink too much.*
*Ain't that the truth?*

*Do you,*
*Do you love me*
*Too?*

I pulled the microphone down before he could even finish the song and answered him in my very best Mariah Carey impersonation. I was totally enchanted by his voice and his lyrics. Nobody— *nobody*—could have pulled that off, except *my* sweetheart, Jason Jones. Whatever spell he casted on me was the same one he had put on me months ago up on that other stage.

"*Yeeeessss … yes, I … do,*" I sang, impressed with myself for being vulnerable and also for admitting feelings that even surprised me a little.

*Maybe this therapy thing is working after all*, I mused.

The crowd erupted into cheers as soon as I finished the song for Jason. Everyone was on their feet, even me, as he took me into his arms and kissed me, front and center. The cheers grew even louder, and I was pretty sure I heard half of Team Jizz in the back, hooting and hollering. I wasn't even embarrassed anymore. I just wanted him to take me home and finally put me up against that damn wall.

"Was that extra enough?" He moved the microphone to the side and smiled down at me.

I could barely hear him over the crowd.

"Plenty." I laughed, blown away by what had just happened.

*Did he really say he loved me? Did I really tell him I loved him back? Did he seriously just tell everyone about my internal fart?*

"Are you sure?" he asked again.

"Yes, I'm sure!"

A sudden *pop* echoed through the air, and confetti—*sparkly* confetti—started to rain down on us. The crowd went wild.

"How about now?" He grinned, knowing he'd already won his prize—me, of course.

"Jason Jones!" I laughed, throwing my arms around him and holding him tight. I rested my cheek against his chest, listening for his heartbeat over the crowd's loud excitement.

*Thump, thump, thump* went his heart.

"That's Mr. Jones," he growled.

*Squeeze and squeeze* went my hooha.

I was falling for him all over again—except, this time, I had to do it the right way. I looked around us at the ambiance, the spotlights, the crowd's standing ovation. I smiled so big that my cheeks hurt as I took it all in. I was falling, he was falling, the confetti was falling. I closed my eyes, filing away another memory that I never wanted to forget.

*Living my best life.*

# Epilogue

## LIZ

It had been six months, and we were still cleaning up sparkly confetti from Deuce's opening-night celebration. Every time I thought I'd found the last piece of sparkle, I would see another one behind a table, under a chair, in my panties. I didn't even know how that piece had gotten there unless it was from Jason's magic wand. He had cast his spell on me with that wand, and I'd done the same back with my awesome personality.

No, really! After that night when he had told me he loved me onstage and we had that long heart-to-heart talk, we had been A-okay. We had both admitted our fuckups, and we'd both admitted to being more open with our feelings moving forward in the future.

As in, we actively practiced our lunchtime mantra to each other, saying, *"Today, I am feeling ..."* fill in the blank.

That way, not only would we not make up bullshit stories in our head, but we could also fulfill each other's needs.

Could you believe it? I, Liz, the queen of bad decisions and manly mistakes, had my brain and my heart on the same page for once. Even my anxiety had miraculously lightened up! It hadn't been easy, and I was still a slow work in progress. But therapy had helped immensely, and it had even helped Jason, who was not only attending therapy now for himself, but he was also attending for us. He'd said he wanted us to do couples therapy before our wedding next summer. We had to squash any issues that might come up, learn to communicate with one another as best we could, and both be on the same page, in the same book. No books in Bosnia.

"Today, I am feeling ... horny," Jason whispered in my ear. He came up behind me, wrapping me in his delicious biceps, discreetly pushing his hard cock into me.

The lunchtime rush finally slowed down, and only a few customers were hanging out, distracted by their laptops.

"Today, I am feeling ...horny too." I giggled quietly as I continued sweeping the floors.

"Then, put that broom down and step into my office. You don't have to do that, you know—the cleaning. The office part, you do have to do. Mr. Jones demands it."

"Okay, boss." I set my broom aside. I didn't mind helping out on my lunch breaks, especially when

Jason fed me bacon and told me I was pretty. It was a small price to pay.

"Oh, I like it when you say that." He grinned back at me, the same grin he'd been giving me for months now. He loved me.

"Do you? Well, I kind of like being the boss's wife. It's like on all those hot porn videos. Boss's wife fucks the pool boy, boss's wife fucks the mailman, boss's wife—"

"No, nope. It won't be anything like that. Boss's wife fucks the boss." He steered me toward the back office.

"Or ... boss's wife fucks the sexy singer. That's you, of course," I said.

His hands on my shoulders were already sending those electric tingles down my spine and into my pants.

"Onstage! We haven't done that one yet!" he said excitedly. Too excitedly.

I wondered how well I would perform doing *that* on a stage. I would admit, I kind of liked the standing ovation I'd had that night I sang to him that I loved him too.

"Let's add it to the list!" I suddenly grew excited about the idea.

We really did have an official fuck list. After I had told Jason the story of how I'd been wanting to get laid up against a wall ever since the first night we'd met, he had sat down and made me make a list of all my fantasies. We had written everything we had ever wanted to try on a sheet of paper and tacked it up on his bedroom wall—the same wall he had fucked me up against, not once, but three times after.

*Check!*

We had made it through about ninety percent of the list—twice already. The last few things we had left would take some effort. Jason had a kink for outer space. Who would have imagined? It was one of those things we had been open and honest about. Being completely vulnerable and baring our souls to each other had come with ousting our kinks, no matter how wild they were. Would I consider flying to outer space to fuck my soon-to-be husband? Hell no. Had I bought an astronaut helmet? Maybe. I was saving that as a special birthday treat.

My phone buzzed in my pocket, interrupting our little love march to his office. Before I checked it, I already knew who it was.

"Again?" Jason asked as he saw me frantically check my text.

"She's just … hormonal." I peeked at my phone, wondering what Jess wanted this time.

> *Jess: Barbeque nachos. Can we get those tomorrow, please? This baby is craving barbeque nachos. Luke said he won't eat any more junk with me because he's putting on sympathy weight! Can you please be my snack bitch? Living your best life, right? YOLO? Today, I'm feeling … hangry!*

I rolled my eyes. Jess's pregnancy was bad for everyone involved. I thought that I might have transferred Ayesha out of my heart and into her womb. Not a day went by that she wasn't asking—no, *demanding* something or other. But we were BFFs after all. And she had helped me get my shit together with Jason and a million times before that … and poor

Luke put up with it all. I owed it to them. They were the best support a friend could ask for. *Team Jizz!*

I texted back.

*Me: Yes, yes. Sure.*

I was happy to help. I really was! Cross my heart.

"I'm guessing she wants pickles and ice cream this time?" Jason asked, pulling me toward him and shutting the door to his office with his foot.

"Such a stereotype! Women who are pregnant don't want that shit! They want bacon and beer! And then they get hangry because they can't have the beer … and then everyone is miserable!" I threw my hands up in mock exasperation.

I really wasn't being worn down by Jess. Not at all. Cross my heart—again. *Team Jizz! Living my best life!*

"What do you think you'll crave when you carry our little Baby Jones?" He tilted my chin up to meet his gaze. He had on his serious face.

We hadn't had this conversation yet. Not seriously anyway. We had only joked here and there about how our baby would have a knack for fancy cheese and farty dogs. Deuce would make an excellent big brother.

"You want kids? Really? Are we having a serious conversation right now, or is this sexy talk?" I stepped back, possibly ruining the moment, but I needed to know. "I'm feeling … nervous."

"I want kids—with you. You're going to be an amazing mom. I'll sing them their lullabies at night, and you'll change their diapers." He grinned.

"Wait a minute now!" I put my hands on my hips.

When I'd said Ayesha was gone, I hadn't really meant it. She would still come out every now and then, even when I was sober these days, but I did have a rein on her at least. Mostly. So ... like I had said, I was a very slow work in progress. At least I hadn't made any more bad decisions—yet.

"I'm kidding! I'm kidding! We'll both sing the lullabies, and we'll both change the diapers—as a team. You know, technically, with our names combined, we could be Team Jizz too. But I don't think that would go over well with pregnant Jess. She might get jealous and cut me into stars." He swiped his finger across his neck and gritted his teeth.

"Mmhmm, she just might." I stepped into him and wedged my index finger between his abs and his jeans, pulling him closer to me. All of this baby talk had me wanting to start trying. I would have Jason's babies any day. That was hot.

"Let's just keep it a secret between us then. We can be Team *Jizzier*." He put his arm around me and brushed back my hair.

I loved it when he touched my hair, especially when he pulled it as he was slamming up against me. Phew, it was getting hot in this tiny closet office.

"I like the sound of that. Team Jizzier in the house!"

"We're going to be the jizziest of jizzes," he teased as his hands wandered down my back and gripped my ass.

"Fo' shizzle dat jizzle, boss." I laughed as I held on to him tightly and put my head on his chest, listening for that familiar heartbeat.

*Thump, thump, thump.*

"Damn, I love you," he whispered, kissing my forehead.

And even after all this time, I still felt the butterflies—fireflies—in my stomach.

*Squeeze and squeeze.*

# Playlist

Did you know *Nashvegas Nights* has an official playlist? Unfortunately, "Stinky Deuce" still isn't available—someone should get on that! But check out the other awesome tunes below! If you'd like, you can listen to the whole playlist on Spotify. Search for Nashvegas Nights by Kat Addams.

"Blank Space" | Taylor Swift

"Doin' It" | LL Cool J

"Falling in Love at a Coffee Shop" | Landon Pigg

"Crazy Bitch" | Buckcherry

"Firefly" | Ed Sheeran

"Why Don't We Get Drunk" | Jimmy Buffett

"Woke Up in Nashville" | Seth Ennis

"Truth Hurts" | Lizzo

"Fix You" | Coldplay

# Acknowledgments

As with everything I do, it's all first and foremost for my daughter. She is my motivation, my laughter, my stop-and-smell-the-roses, and my world. I am so grateful for her and all of my family who have supported me throughout my endless hours with my door closed and my head in the laptop. Thank you all for feeding yourselves sometimes so that I could meet a deadline!

My writing wouldn't be the same without my dream team. My editor, Jovana Shirley, puts my English degree to shame and makes way too much sense sometimes. My cover designer, Lori Jackson, not only skillfully designs the most swoonworthy covers, but she's also one of the most helpful and genuine people that I've met in this industry. My PR wonder woman, Kelley Jefferson, always tells me like it is and guides me where I need to go. Thank you so much to these wonderful ladies who make writing even more of a dream come true for me!

Thank you to all of my dedicated readers. I always feel like this is old and worn-out when authors do this, but it's so true. Readers are what keep us authors going. Your excitement is what motivates us. Anytime an author gets a good review or a reader reaches out and tells us how much they enjoy our books, we are beyond thrilled. We might do a happy dance in the kitchen or a cartwheel down the hall. We love to hear from you! Seriously, give yourselves a big pat on the back because you all rock!

Lastly, thank you to me—for being me and doing me. That goes for everybody. Be kind to yourself, do something for yourself, believe in yourself. You are loved, valued, and worth it. Even if you have to start over a hundred times, you'll get there one day. Exhale the bullshit and keep on going. You're all queens, so put on your crowns and stand up.

the regular. That's some other romance author. The poor thing probably has to sneak away upstairs to write her dirty stories! What would her family think? Thankfully, that's not Kat!

Social Media:

Still crazy about Kat? Rawr! Stalk her on the social media platforms linked below!

https://linktr.ee/author_kat_addams
(For all of the links in one convenient location!)

Newsletter: www.kataddams.com/subscribe
(Bonus *Hotty Toddy* Free E-Book)

www.goodreads.com/author/show/
19253462.Kat_Addams

www.bookbub.com/profile/kat-addams

http://amazon.com/author/kataddams

Kat's Kittens:
www.facebook.com/groups/651192492026240/
(A Facebook group to stay connected, laugh, and share. Hope to see you there!)

www.facebook.com/KatAddamsAuthor

www.instagram.com/authorkataddams

https://twitter.com/KatAddamsAuthor

Want to keep up with all the mischief and bad decisions? Be sure to subscribe to Kat's newsletter for the latest news, including a special Ask Team Jizz advice column! You can find her newsletter on her website: www.kataddams.com/subscribe. By becoming a subscriber, you'll be the first to know the juicy details on upcoming releases—hello, Dirty South, Book 3! You'll also be the first to hear of special offers, exclusive content, sneak peeks, terrible ideas, ridiculous shenanigans, and more! As a special gift for signing up, you'll also receive a free e-book, *Hotty Toddy*. Check below for more information on this stand-alone, second-chance, and fake marriage novella.

# OTHER BOOKS BY KAT ADDAMS

COMING SOON!

MR. BIG ~~EASY~~ EGO,
DIRTY SOUTH SERIES, BOOK 3.

AVAILABLE SOON FOR
PREORDER ON AMAZON.

OFFICIALLY LAUNCHING FEBRUARY 2020.

AVAILABLE NOW!

*Grit and Grind, Dirty South Series, Book 1*
*Available on Amazon.*

Klara Woods is an aspiring writer ... with no inspiration. After one too many disastrous relationships, her quest for a leading man has fizzled out. Bored with her mundane lifestyle, she decides to do whatever it takes to get her head back in the game. When she finds out that one of her favorite authors, Christopher Kaiser, is leading a writers workshop, she's the first in line to sign up. Could he help spark her creativity again, or will this be just another one of her bad decisions?

Christopher Kaiser is an international best-selling author whose books have taken the romance genre by storm. Rumor has it that his sexy stories are inspired by personal experiences with his many so-called muses. Touted as one of the South's most notorious playboys, Christopher is too busy living his best life to settle down anytime soon. Besides, what would happen with his writing if he gave up his "explorations"?

Determined to take matters into her own hands, Klara decides to jump-start her love life with a catastrophe of her own making. Unfortunately, an innocent bystander prevents her desperate attempt for attention by rescuing her from yet another one of her bad decisions. Annoyed—and also a bit turned on by this sexy new hero—Klara goes home, defeated. Forcing herself to focus on her writing, she shows up to her first workshop and quickly learns that her hero from earlier is none other than her instructor, Christopher Kaiser. Will she actually learn something from this, or will she be too distracted by her hots for the teacher?

Jules Turner is all about peace, love, and light. She's always marched to the beat of her own drum, even when that beat took her far from her hometown of Oxford, Mississippi, and straight to sunny California. For the past ten years, she has been perfectly content to trade in her Southern roots for a yoga mat and herbal tea.

When her meddlesome mother suddenly interrupts Jules's namaste life by asking her to return for a visit, Jules knows her mom is probably scheming to play matchmaker ... again. She won't fall for it this time though ... except that she does—literally—landing right at the feet of her former flame.

Todd Miller—aka Hotty Toddy—is just as ruggedly gorgeous as he was in high school. When he learns that his teenage crush is back in town—and just in time for their ten-year reunion—he convinces Jules to come up with some scheming of their own. If Todd is lucky, their scheming will take them straight to the bedroom, where he tried—and failed—to seduce Jules on prom night so many years ago.

Pretending to be happily married, Todd and Jules strike out to fool their old high school bullies in the ultimate prank. But they quickly learn that they're really just fooling themselves. They can't just *pretend*. Not when they can't keep their hands off of each other.

How can two people who have been apart for so long connect again so quickly? What happens if their fake romance turns into something real? Will Todd be able to handle Jules's free-spirited adventures in California, or can he convince her to stay back in Mississippi and embrace her small-town roots?

With a little bit of scheming—okay, *a lot* of scheming—Jules just might find that her matchmaking mother knows best.